"You, Felicity Barrett, are unfinished business."

Seth's eyes blazed with a strange intensity. "And I like to finish what I start."

It took Felicity a moment to regain her composure. She was rapidly losing control of this conversation—and of herself. "Thank you for dinner, Seth." She noticed that her voice wasn't as firm as she wished. "See you tomorrow?"

He nodded. "I'll be working on the stagecoach commercial, too."

He was still alarmingly close and Felicity felt her heartbeat quicken. But before she could decide what to say next, Seth gave a slow smile and pulled her hard against his chest, kissing her with lips that tantalized, tasted and lingered wantonly on hers. Then he drew away.

"I . . ." Felicity stammered. *It was only a kiss,* she told herself angrily. "Good night, Seth," she finally managed.

But Seth didn't leave. His hand brushed her cheek as he said, very softly, "Be careful on the set tomorrow, okay?"

Felicity suddenly felt uneasy. *Why did he say that?*

Dear Reader,

As a native of Colorado, I love writing about my home state. In fact, *Unlikely Places* is my second Colorado Romance; the first—*An Unlikely Combination* (Harlequin Romance 2918)—was published in July, 1988.

Silverton, the town in this story, is a very real community, a delightful scenic resort in the Rocky Mountains. However, the Department of Tourism and its commercials, and the saboteurs and skulduggery that occur in *Unlikely Places* are purely fictitious. And while it's true that Silverton is an active mining town, there is no uranium mining there at present. (Despite my fabrications, though, the possibility of mineral deposits does exist. Much of the Rockies remains unexplored to this day.)

When you read *Unlikely Places*, I hope you'll agree that Silverton is a perfect setting for romance!

Anne Marie Duquette

UNLIKELY PLACES

Anne Marie Duquette

Harlequin Books

TORONTO • NEW YORK • LONDON
AMSTERDAM • PARIS • SYDNEY • HAMBURG
STOCKHOLM • ATHENS • TOKYO • MILAN

ISBN 0-373-03080-0

Harlequin Romance first edition October 1990

With many thanks to
Peggy Weber Zachary
for her friendship and invaluable assistance

CHAPTER ONE

"LADIES, LADIES, that was terrible! That was more like a funeral than a commercial! How about putting a little life into your performance?"

Felicity Barrett listened to the director's words with dismay. True, she was just a walk-on actress, and an inexperienced one at that, but she thought she'd handled her part as an 1860s saloon girl quite well.

The director, who was known to everyone as simply Bill, shook his head and approached the pine boardwalk in front of the century-old saloon where the filming was taking place.

"How many of you extras are local?"

Eight of the ten saloon girls, Felicity included, raised their hands. Technically, Felicity wasn't a local. She was away from home on an unwanted break from her job and had jumped at the chance to be an extra to relieve the boredom. The state of Colorado was filming tourist commercials advertising this tiny mountain town of Silverton, and Felicity was lucky to have been chosen for a part.

"How many of you have never acted before?" Bill continued.

Six other hands remained in the air besides hers, Felicity noticed.

Bill shook his head in dismay. "I'm sorry to say your inexperience definitely shows. Remember, you're all saloon girls on the prowl for a man! It's Silverton in the 1860s, boom-town days. The miners are rich with silver profits, and you want to celebrate their good fortune with them. For a price, of course," he emphasized.

A few of the young women giggled.

"Look at yourselves," Bill ordered. "In those costumes, you want men to be hungry for your love!"

Felicity glanced down at the scanty, flame-red satin dress she wore. Her shoulders were bare, with her normally proportioned bustline pushed into eye-catching prominence by the tight lacing of the bodice. Her small, fine-boned frame had grown, thanks to three-inch black heels, while her normally straight brunette hair sported tiny ringlets and bows instead of its usual blunt nononsense cut. And the hazel eyes flecked with green were heavily made up into a come-hither look.

"I want all of you to get into character! Pick out a man from the scene and focus your eyes on him, then ooze sexiness from every pore! Remember, people, the light is fading. We only have time for one more take." Bill gave them all an encouraging thumbs-up, then headed back to his position behind the cameras. "Ten seconds now," he announced. "Everyone in their places."

Felicity quickly positioned herself in front of the saloon doors. Look sexy, Bill had told them. That was easier said than done. Her busy job back in Portland with the family shipping business didn't leave much time for practicing feminine wiles.

Felicity desperately looked at the other Western-costumed men, seeking a target for inspiration. Her eyes scanned and discarded them, then immediately zeroed in on a man in street clothes standing behind the cameras. She had noticed this man before. There was something about him, a magnetism that seemed to draw Felicity, even from a distance. Perhaps it was his easy vitality or his enthusiasm for his work, but whatever it was, he stood out from the rest of the crowd.

He seemed to be some sort of adviser to Bill, although he didn't look like one of the regular crew from the Colorado Department of Tourism. His clothes were casual and comfortable, not tight and faddish like theirs, but they still revealed a trim, proportioned body.

Felicity let her gaze wander with saloon-girl wantonness over the man. A tingle of excitement shot through her, jolting her with surprise. Was this what acting was all about? she wondered as she continued her performance. She pursed her lips appealingly, her eyes now on his face. It wasn't a classically handsome face, but with its rough planes and angles it was attractive all the same.

Still, that first impression of ruggedness was softened by the blue eyes beneath the dark brown hair, which spoke of humor and intelligence. Felicity wished he'd turn them her way, which would make her job easier. Acting without an audience was difficult, she'd discovered. The man was occupied with his clipboard full of notes.

"All right, everyone. Ready... action!"

Blair Street in Silverton, Colorado, came alive. Riders on horseback passed in front of the cameras, while the saloon girls made enticing movements toward the male actors on the pine boardwalks.

Felicity felt her body uncoil, stage nervousness being replaced by feminine allure as she pretended to offer herself to the tall, blue-eyed man next to Bill. She wrapped a slim arm around one of the saloon's support posts and casually leaned against it, her eyes suggesting promises soon to be fulfilled.

Inside the saloon, a cue was given, and a rowdy fight began. Two miners came crashing through the saloon's swinging doors, and the saloon girls gave their mock screams of fear. All, that is, except Felicity.

The man with the blue eyes had turned Felicity's way. She started as their eyes suddenly locked, and the immediate embarrassment she felt at being caught boldly ogling made her lose character and freeze.

"You in the red! Watch the fight! Watch the fight!" Bill screamed at her, but the words didn't register.

The man was now smiling in open amusement. Felicity could tell he knew he'd been singled out as a pretend client. Her cheeks flushed, but despite her embarrassment she managed to tilt her chin in the air and return his look. Her eyes let him know she was only doing her job.

"You in the red! Pay attention!" the megaphone blasted out, and Felicity finally realized that it was directed at her. She hurriedly turned her attention back to the fight. Unfortunately, her high heel stuck in a knothole of the old-fashioned pine sidewalk, and she teetered off balance.

For one awful second she clawed at the nearby post. Her grasping fingers missed it by a fraction of an inch, then she fell backward, landing on her behind with a resounding thump. The surrounding mountains and all of Blair Street were treated to an array of white petticoats and trim legs.

"Cut!" Bill ordered furiously.

The action stopped, and all eyes turned toward the figure on the ground. Felicity tried to pull her foot loose, but the heel was solidly wedged in. Her cheeks flushed even redder as she looked up and saw that Blue Eyes was fighting hard to hold back a laugh. She ducked her head, the corkscrew curls of her period hairstyle bobbing ridiculously as she reached for the tiny buckles that fastened the shoe.

"She ruined the last take of the day!" Felicity heard Bill groan. "A whole day's worth of filming wasted!"

"I'm sorry. It was an accident," Felicity rushed to explain to those around her. The other saloon girls tried to help, all the extra fingers making it impossible for anyone to effectively get at the buckles.

Felicity remained on her rear end, her foot uninjured but tucked and trapped beneath her. Just when she thought things couldn't get any worse, she saw denim-covered, muscled legs part the sea of nylon-clad, high-heeled ones. Felicity looked straight up at the object of her first disastrous attempt at method acting.

"Are you all right?" The deep voice from above was alive with mirth.

Felicity realized with a shock that her strapless dress had fallen alarmingly low, exposing cleavage that would have done a real saloon girl proud—and giving him a perfect view. Biting her lip, she clutched at her bodice and yanked it up to a more discreet level.

"I'm just fine," was her clipped answer. "Only I'm stuck." Felicity smoothed out her skirt, trying to rearrange the mass of petticoats and flounces that were hiked high on her thighs.

"Hmmm. So I see." He examined the position of her trapped leg, then motioned for everyone to stand back. "May I suggest you hold on to your . . ." He paused, and gave the vast expanse of her bare skin an appreciative look. "The best chance we have of getting you loose is if I lift you up onto your feet," he said.

He reached down, and Felicity immediately grabbed the top of her dress with both hands.

"Are you ready? Here we go." Two large hands slid under Felicity's arms, and she was easily lifted to a standing position.

"Hold on to me while I try to free your foot," the man said, but before she could do so, Bill interrupted.

"Is she okay, Seth?" Bill asked in a worried voice, his earlier disappointment over blowing a take obviously replaced by fears of injuries and insurance claims.

"For now," Seth replied, much to Bill's relief. He bent over, reached for Felicity's ankle, and yanked the troublesome shoe loose. "But I can't make any promises for the future. Just look at this!"

He held out the shoe for Bill to inspect, with Felicity's foot still in it. "I told you before, saloon girls in the 1800s didn't wear sheer nylons. They wore black stockings and black boots. Not," he said with distaste, "high heels. It's your own fault this shoot was ruined, Bill, not hers."

"Do you mind?" Felicity asked indignantly, tightening her hold on his neck and tottering on one high-heeled shoe. "I feel like a piece of beef on the inspection block."

Both men ignored her.

"I don't know why you're paying me to be a technical consultant if you aren't going to take my advice. You said you wanted these commercials to be historically accurate," Felicity's captor told Bill in a reasonable voice.

"Excuse me!" Felicity tried again.

"I do want accuracy," Bill muttered.

Felicity gave a great yank and finally succeeded in jerking her foot free from Seth's hand. She removed her arms from the man's neck, but his arm was still around her waist for support.

"Then get rid of the heels! You'll be representing the time period far more accurately." For the first time Seth turned his full attention to Felicity. "It might even save this young woman a few broken bones."

Felicity blinked with surprise at the concern in his voice.

"All right, all right." The director threw Felicity one last, accusing look, then addressed the crowd. "I want you all back here at six tomorrow morning. You saloon girls, see wardrobe before then to be fitted for boots."

"And black stockings," Seth added, gesturing toward Felicity's legs.

"And stockings." Bill sighed, and Seth nodded, apparently satisfied.

Bill left, and Felicity, who had given up trying to escape, waited with resignation for her release. Finally the strong arm was moved from her waist and held out toward her by way of introduction.

"Pleased to meet you, ma'am."

Felicity nodded and took his hand, torn between wanting to flee all the curious spectators and meeting her rescuer. She decided to stay, just for a moment. "I'm Felicity Barrett. Thanks for the help."

"You're welcome. I'm Daniel Seth Tyler. But everyone calls me Seth. I'm a junior," he explained. "My father goes by Dan."

Felicity gave him a polite smile and a businesslike handshake. "It's nice to meet you. Now if you'll excuse me, I really should change and get back to my room."

"So soon? I wanted to ask how you like our town." The question in his deep baritone wasn't a polite, superficial one. Felicity could see that he seemed very interested in her answer.

She looked around at the mountains ringing the town, the harsh peaks of the San Juan Range softened by the passing clouds. Their light granite was covered by a vast variety of aspen and evergreen, and the majestic peaks, some 14,000 feet high and perpetually covered with snow, left her with a feeling of awe. There were no mountains like these back in Portland.

"I love it," she said reverently. "How could I not?"

Her simple answer seemed to please Seth immensely. "I'm glad. Some people don't."

Felicity could tell that she had just passed some kind of test, but instead of being annoyed, she felt happy that this man had not found her wanting. "It's gorgeous here. Just beautiful," she added. And she meant it.

Seth gave her a brilliant smile. "Why don't I buy you a cup of coffee? I'm a resident, by the way, and I know all the best places."

Felicity hesitated. His offer was tempting; in fact, it was very tempting, especially since Seth hadn't referred to her clumsy fall or worse, her use of him as a fantasy lover for her saloon-girl character. She appreciated that, but still...

"I'd better not. I'm very tired. I think I'll just get something to read and go to bed early."

Seth nodded his understanding. "Living this high in the mountains seems to tire most newcomers. Some extra sleep will help prevent that, and our high-altitude headaches, too."

Felicity smiled gratefully. She had indeed been having headaches, but she knew they weren't induced by the altitude. This vacation hadn't been her idea. It was a result of parental pressure, her doctor's orders, and a very heavy work schedule that had left her burned out from the stresses and demands of the family business.

"That's good to know," Felicity said. "I'll try to get some extra rest."

"Glad to be of service. If there's anything else I can do for you, let me know."

"Perhaps you could direct me to a drugstore before you go? I'd like to buy a newspaper," she explained, not wanting him to think she needed something for high-altitude problems. She had her own headache prescription in her room.

"I can walk you there myself."

Felicity welcomed Seth's offer. She found his company appealing, and it was with definite regret that she said, "I really have to go change out of this outfit." She surreptitiously checked to see that the bodice of her dress was still at a decent level. "And I need to see the wardrobe mistress about getting boots for tomorrow. It might take a while. You probably won't want to wait."

"I have plenty of time." Seth smiled again—engagingly.

Felicity couldn't help but smile back. "Are all the residents here as friendly as you?"

"Of course we are, especially with good-looking outsiders." Seth hooked his thumbs in his jeans and casually leaned back against one of the wooden posts. They were spaced at frequent intervals, all supporting the edges of the roofs that extended to form a protective cover for the pine-planked sidewalk.

"After all," he went on, "there are only about eight hundred permanent residents in Silverton. Take out the young and the old, the married and the committed, and that doesn't leave us single men with a very big dating pool. If I don't ask you out first, some other bachelor will."

Felicity blinked at his outspokenness. "You're serious, aren't you?"

"I certainly am."

"Aren't you seeing someone?" she asked bluntly, determined to make sure she wasn't headed for trouble. She made it a point to avoid attached men.

"There's been no one for a long time." The words were spoken casually, but with a definite air of finality. "I can promise you—no wives, children or old girlfriends popping out of nowhere. So, how about that cup of coffee with me?"

Felicity hesitated, but not because she was tired. She wanted to be with him more than their short acquaintance warranted, and she wondered how wise it would be to follow up on such uncharacteristic urges.

Seth must have noticed her hesitation. "Before you refuse, remember who rescued your shoe from a pine-splintered demise."

Felicity remembered how Seth had confronted Bill in her defense, and how he had argued for safer shoes for all the actresses. Then she suddenly remembered the feel of his hands as he'd effortlessly lifted her to her feet.

"All right, I'll have that coffee," she decided. Her eyes sparkled with excitement. "I'll try not to be too long." Felicity hurried toward the building rented by the government film crew for wardrobe changes.

It was a rare treat to meet someone who didn't travel in the same business and social circles she did. How long had it been since she'd seen a man who wasn't a carbon copy of all her other dates? Somehow it had seemed easier, even preferable, to forgo many of those routine, boring dates for the entrenched discipline of her position as president of marketing and sales with Barrett Shipping back in Portland.

Unfortunately her preference for the excitement of business over the dullness of her social life had only added to a workload that was already heavy. Felicity

Barrett was a full-fledged workaholic. Even bad health and a forced vacation hadn't slowed her down.

That was why she was trying her hand at acting. Her doctor had told her that only complete rest would cure her headaches; standing around in costume couldn't possibly hurt her number-weary brain. And the fact that she was once again productive satisfied the burning drive, the deeply ingrained urge to be constantly occupied.

The paycheck certainly meant nothing. She didn't need this money—wouldn't need it—even if the vacation here *hadn't* already been planned and paid for by her mother. In Colorado, Felicity's oldest brother, Miles, and his wife, Sherri, were expecting their first child. They were the only Barretts who lived outside Portland, so Felicity's mother had planned to sight-see in Silverton while she awaited the birth of her next grandchild.

Felicity's mental exhaustion had changed those plans, and a reluctant Felicity had been forced on the plane instead. Insisting she didn't want to leave the family business shorthanded, yet knowing that she couldn't stand many more of the pounding headaches that were occurring with increasing frequency, Felicity had given in. But she hadn't relented completely. She was not spending her vacation lounging in some hotel.

When she arrived in Silverton, she'd noticed signs advertising for walk-on actresses, and had immediately applied for the job. Bill had been most accommodating when she approached him; he'd even specified in her contract that she was to be released from work as soon as she was notified of the baby's birth. After all, she wouldn't be needed for more than two weeks, Bill had said, and her role was minor.

Although Felicity had ignored her doctor's advice to rest completely, she didn't feel a bit guilty. She had a job that was keeping her happily busy, and now she even had an actual date with an interesting man, someone other than the business-suited, briefcase-toting, run-of-the-mill executive types she usually encountered.

"Hurry back, now!" Seth called out as she turned toward an alley.

Felicity waved, then rounded the corner to get to the outdoor stairs, which led to the second floor of the wooden building. She stopped abruptly, nearly losing her balance again on the high heels. In the alley closest to the saloon were two old men, and their hands held the leashes of four very large dogs.

"Uh, excuse me. I need to get past your dogs so I can go upstairs."

The men started guiltily, looking as surprised to see Felicity as she was to see them. They said nothing, however, and made no motion to move. One of the dogs barked, and Felicity decided she wasn't moving, either. In fact, she was suddenly glad of the leashes fastened to the collars. All the dogs looked formidable.

"Are you waiting for someone?" she asked. "Are you with the film crew?"

"Yes. That's it. We're with the film crew," one of the men said, his voice hoarse and cracked with age. "We're um, in charge of the dogs for the commercials." He gave the other man a quick, affirming look.

"Oh. Well, you might as well leave. Bill said we're all done with shooting for today. I'm here to change," Felicity explained, gesturing at the wardrobe building.

The two men again exchanged quick, peculiar glances. Then, while Felicity waited, they led the animals out of the narrow alleyway, leaving her path clear.

Strange, Felicity thought, but then everything about the film industry seemed strange to her. It was all so new.

She ran up the stairs to change into jeans and a heavy sweater, and to cream off the stage makeup. Her casual clothes were a welcome change from her everyday business suits, and she almost decided against putting on a normal application of makeup. After all, she was on vacation. But then, she *was* going out for coffee with the very appealing Seth Tyler. A trace of eye shadow and mascara wouldn't hurt.

The corkscrew curls looked ridiculous on her now, so she combed them out into a smoother mass of brunette waves that just brushed her shoulders. Goodbye, saloon girl; hello, regular old Felicity. She wondered if Seth Tyler would still be interested in her without the actress trimmings.

She was fairly attractive, but she was certainly no saloon vamp or great beauty. Felicity inspected her face in the mirror. The faint shadows under her eyes from overwork were still there, but the makeup helped, and the soft waves were a pleasant alternative to her usual straight hairstyle.

"That was quick," Seth remarked as she rejoined him. "You don't look at all like you did when I first saw you."

Felicity stiffened.

"You look even better," he said, and Felicity relaxed at the compliment.

"I do prefer this to flashing petticoats and..." She hesitated.

"A dress at half-mast?" Seth led her around the corner of Blair Street over to Main.

"It wasn't that bad," Felicity protested.

"No, it certainly wasn't," Seth murmured, a look of masculine admiration in his eyes.

"I thought you only noticed my historical inaccuracies," Felicity said tartly, secretly flattered.

"Your high heels were the main topic of conversation," Seth admitted, "but they could only hold my interest for so long."

Felicity's cheeks warmed, and she quickly decided to change the subject. "You promised to show me where the drugstore is."

"We're headed there now. I'm glad to see you're wearing sensible walking shoes," he said, glancing at her almost-new sneakers. "Most of us locals don't do much driving around town."

"Why? Because of the road conditions?" Felicity knew that only some of Silverton's streets were paved. Some were still dirt roads, just as they must have been a century ago, she supposed.

"No, it's just quicker to walk where you want to go than drive. We aren't very big."

"What with the dirt roads and the boardwalks, everything looks so old here," Felicity observed.

"Everything *is* old. Many of the original buildings erected during the silver-boom days in the 1860s still exist. They're still used today. There aren't many period recreations. Sometimes I forget how all this looks to an outsider. It's just home to me. You prefer the city, I suppose." His voice had taken on a slight edge she hadn't noticed before.

"Well, the city is 'just home' to me, you know. As beautiful as Silverton is, it's not what I'm used to. I don't often take vacations. Under ordinary circumstances, this would be a pretty unlikely place for me to visit. Don't you have any, er, friends who aren't from around here?" Felicity asked, anxious to hear Seth's answer. She'd be so disappointed if he turned out to be one of those closed-minded people who rejected anything unfamiliar.

"Not really. I used to believe that people of similar backgrounds had the best chance at happiness, but . . ." Seth shrugged. "I'm not an expert. It's hard to say."

Felicity thought of all the men she had dated who shared her background—wealthy, intelligent city men on their way up in the world. "The theory seems sound," she finally said, "but associating only with people like yourself can be awfully boring."

Seth looked at her, startled. "I guess it can, at that. But it's hard to change. I can't imagine myself moving to the city just to meet new people. How about you?"

"If I did move to a small town, I suppose I'd get used to it," she said politely.

Privately, Felicity didn't think she ever could. The slow pace, the lack of excitement and opportunities, would just be too stultifying after a while. And she found living in a century-old time warp definitely unsettling. Give her Barrett Shipping and the hustle and bustle of Portland any day. Still, meeting a new man *not* from Portland wouldn't be amiss. . . .

Seth led her into the drugstore, a place that obviously catered more to locals than tourists.

A friendly chorus of "Hi, Seth" greeted them, and Seth stopped to chat with everyone after showing Felicity the news rack. She passed up the local papers—the *Denver Post* and the *Rocky Mountain News*—for the *Wall Street Journal,* a *U.S. News and World Report* and a *Businessman's Weekly.* For a small town, the selection was quite good.

Perhaps tonight she could read without getting one of her pounding headaches. Just looking at her trade journals at the airport in Portland had sent her reaching for the painkillers the doctor had prescribed.

"Ready?" Seth asked, appearing at her side the instant she'd finished making her selections, despite protests from his neighbors to linger awhile.

Felicity nodded. Making her way to the cash register, she wondered what it would be like to be as well-known as Seth apparently was. She couldn't even boast of being recognized by most people at work, and she was the owner's daughter. Of course, that was her own fault for staying cooped up in her office so much.

"Afternoon, Seth," said the lady at the cash register. Her hair was white, her face wrinkled, but her voice was full of life.

"You're looking terribly attractive today, Flo," Seth said to the woman as she rang up Felicity's purchases.

"And you're lying more than usual today, Seth," the woman dryly replied, although a slight twinkle flashed in the wise old eyes. "Are you going to introduce me to your friend, or don't you remember the manners your mother taught you?"

Seth heaved a long-suffering sigh, but his face was kind. "Flo, this is Felicity Barrett. She's with the government film crew from the state tourism department. Felicity, meet Flo. She owns this little store, and tries not to cheat us too much."

As he spoke, he added a small book on the history of Silverton to Felicity's selections. "This should help you capture the feeling of the town a hundred years ago," he said. "It'll fill in some of the lesser-known details." He reached for his wallet with the obvious intention of paying for her purchases.

"I can pay," Felicity said. "Really."

"Let her pay, Seth," Flo agreed. "Authors aren't supposed to buy their own books."

"You wrote this?" Felicity picked up the small book, and saw that it did indeed carry Seth Tyler's name.

"He's an historian, and a darn good one, too. That's why he was hired to advise on those tourist commercials. He knows this area as well as the old-timers do. We're all very proud of him," Flo boasted.

Felicity turned to gaze at Seth. Good looks *and* brains, she thought with new interest. Giving a deprecatory shrug, he pulled several bills from his wallet and held them out to Flo.

"If that's the case, I certainly will pay," Felicity insisted. She placed her own money on the counter.

"Wait." Flo plucked another book from the paperback carousel and tossed it onto the pile. "Seth's history book is very good, but this other stuff of yours looks pretty dull, Miss. Here, read this. Compliments of the store."

Felicity inspected the new addition. "This is fiction. Thank you for the offer, but I never read fiction."

"Never?" Seth asked curiously.

Felicity shook her head. "No. I stick mostly to trade journals and business publications. Besides," she added, studying the cover, then turning it over and scanning the blurb, "even if I did read fiction, I'd certainly never read cowboy stories. They don't interest me in the least."

"I think they're properly called Westerns," Seth gently corrected her, his voice faintly amused.

"Whatever." She glanced at the author's name. "I've never heard of this Decker Townsend. I'll bet his stories are as phony as his pen name. Thank you, Flo, but I think I'll pass."

Flo took the book from her hand, then stubbornly slapped it down on the counter. "Everyone says Decker Townsend is the next Louis L'Amour. And we *like*

Westerns here in Silverton. For your information, Bat Masterson was once our sheriff. We don't turn up our noses at our heritage.''

"I'm sorry. I really didn't mean to offend," Felicity said stiffly, deciding that the wisest course would be to count out the extra money. Flo was evidently determined that she take the book, and Felicity didn't want a scene. She probably should have graciously accepted it when she had the chance. Besides, she could always give it away later.

Once outside, Seth suggested they walk to a nearby coffee shop, then said, "Flo can be a little forceful at times, but I know she thought you'd enjoy the book. Still, you certainly don't have to read it if you don't want. Give it to me, and I'll reimburse you."

"No, I couldn't do that," Felicity told him. "I'll keep the book. It's just that I'm more interested in learning about the history of Silverton than in reading a Western."

Seth seemed more puzzled than pleased by her enthusiasm. "I thought you already knew quite a bit about this town. Didn't your production agency fill you in on Silverton's background?"

Felicity shook her head. "Oh, no. I hardly know anything about Silverton at all."

Seth came to an abrupt halt. "You mean they didn't tell you a thing about this town? I assumed Bill's regular workers would have been acquainted with our history as part of their preparation for the commercials."

"They probably are. But Seth, I'm not one of Bill's regular workers. I never worked for the Colorado Department of Tourism until I arrived here this week."

Seth's face immediately changed from one of friendly interest to cold hostility.

Bewildered, Felicity asked, "What's wrong?"

"I thought you were a member of the regular crew from Denver. I had no idea you were the kind of person who'd take food from the mouths of children."

CHAPTER TWO

"WHAT ARE YOU talking about?" Felicity asked, blinking with surprise at his sudden change of mood.

"Don't act dumb with me," Seth snapped. "If you aren't a regular member of Bill's crew, then you must have been hired as a local."

"Well, yes, I was," Felicity stammered. "But I don't see the harm in that. I was on vacation, and I saw the sign advertising for walk-on actresses, so I applied."

That answer only made Seth angrier. "You mean to tell me you have a *regular* job?" he demanded.

"Of course."

"Is it a well-paying job?" Seth's eyes narrowed unpleasantly.

"I suppose you could say that," Felicity replied. "I work for a family-owned company, so my salary's quite generous. Is there something wrong with that?" she asked, still wondering why she was being interrogated.

Seth made a sound of disbelief. "Yes, there certainly is! You're passing yourself off as a local, and taking away a potential salary from one of our residents, a salary that you don't even need! What kind of woman takes another job on vacation, anyway?"

Felicity couldn't believe the force of his attack. "There's no law against a person taking on a second job," she said indignantly. "And there was no deception involved on my part. I didn't pretend to be a local when

I was hired. I even put my home address of Portland on the job application.''

Felicity saw that her explanation hadn't calmed Seth at all. She didn't know why she was bothering to defend herself to him, but for some reason she wanted his good opinion. And she resented this slight on her integrity.

''If you knew anything at all,'' Seth muttered irritably, ''you'd know that our merchant economy is based on the summer tourism business.''

''Why is it so important that only locals work on these commercials? I'm sure my working here for a few weeks won't make much difference one way or the other.''

''That's where you're wrong! Silverton closes up with the first big snowfall. Most of our merchants live year-round on the income they make in the summer.''

''There . . . there aren't any other jobs for people once winter comes?'' Felicity asked incredulously.

''So it's finally sinking in.'' Seth's voice was scornful. ''Once the snows hit, the railway and most of the roads into Silverton are inaccessible. That's the end of the tourists, and the end of any jobs except at a few old mines that are still being worked.''

''How can any place be so cut off from the rest of the world?'' Felicity asked. ''With all the modern technology available there must—''

''Modern technology hasn't figured out a way to stop tons of snow from falling. Look around you!'' Seth gestured toward the surrounding peaks. ''We're nine thousand feet above sea level! It never gets hot here. On the higher peaks, the snow remains all year long. You try keeping a railway line open and roads cleared when there's ten or twenty feet of snow over them.''

Seth exhaled wearily. ''Don't you see, Felicity? This town would never have existed in the first place if it wasn't for the silver discovered here, and it would never have remained alive after the miners left if it wasn't for the tourists. If every tourist who came here *took* from our source of income instead of *contributing* to it, we'd soon become just another ghost town. That's why these commercials are so important. Silverton needs the income.''

''I'm really sorry,'' Felicity said sincerely. ''I had no idea. If I could, I'd get out of my contract, but I don't think they'll consider not being a resident a good-enough reason.''

Seth snorted in derision. ''You should have thought of that earlier.''

''I don't need the money. I could always contribute my paychecks to the town,'' Felicity said impulsively. ''I'm sure one of your churches or seniors centers could use them.''

That was the wrong thing to say.

''We don't want charity. All we want is an opportunity to earn a living without any interference from people like you. If you'll excuse me, I have to be going.''

Felicity hated seeing Seth go down the dirt road, puffs of dust flying with every angry stride. She sighed with disappointment, then grimaced as she felt the beginnings of another headache. After a moment she turned and walked back to her room.

Felicity was staying at the Grand Imperial Hotel, which had been in business since 1882. She'd chosen to stay there because the original interior had been restored to its earlier Victorian splendor.

But now she was in no mood to appreciate the nineteenth-century brass bed, the oak water tank in her room, or the period wallpaper. Her head was throbbing, and the day that had started so pleasantly had come to a discordant end. Such an unusual man, and such an unusual town, Felicity thought as she took a tablet for her headache and lay down on the bed.

If only she was back home again. Felicity thought longingly of her town house. She'd moved out of the Barrett family home shortly after her promotion to head of marketing, but she'd made certain to purchase a place in the same neighborhood. Those evenings alone with her spread sheets could get a little too lonely.

At least back in Portland, she knew how to act and what to expect. But her family would have a fit if she returned early. Her father, Frank Barrett, and her brother, Roger, had sworn that the firm could manage without her for a while—even though it was summer, the busiest time for logging along the Columbia River. Her young assistant, a distant Barrett cousin with a brand-new MBA, had been eager to prove his worth and take on more of her responsibilities. Felicity knew the company barges would be overbooked, and she wished she was back in her office doing her job.

Her mother would certainly have put a stop to that, though. Emily Barrett had been the one to force Felicity to see the doctor when her headaches had become too severe to hide any longer. The family doctor, aware of Felicity's background, had taken one look at her and immediately suspended her from work. The company had been her life since she was seventeen years old, even while attending high school and college. Ten years without a proper vacation was far too long, he'd emphasized. Felicity wasn't to work until further notice.

Felicity had rebelled with the stubbornness that was characteristic of her whole family. She loved the nuts and bolts of the business, delighted in the technical aspects of buying and selling, and carrying out major business deals was her joy in life. In fact, her father had often remarked that she should have been the oldest son instead of the youngest, and only, daughter.

Unfortunately for Frank, Roger Barrett, the second oldest, was only interested in piloting the company barges. The oldest son, Miles, had left the company years before, much to his father's disappointment. He'd married in Colorado and had settled there permanently.

Because of this, Felicity had been allowed to assume more and more responsibility at Barrett Shipping. With her father's blessing, she'd become the heir apparent. Eventually she had worked her way up to her present position as president of marketing and sales. But it appeared that her weary body, especially her traitorous head, couldn't keep pace with her busy, active brain.

Felicity rubbed at her temples. If only that pill would start working! But the doctor had warned her that her physical problems were a direct result of emotional stress. She would have to sort out her priorities, make some changes to her demanding business schedule, before the headaches were banished permanently, he had explained.

"What does he know?" Felicity grumbled aloud, reaching for the *Wall Street Journal*.

Ten minutes later her head was really pounding, and Felicity cursed the medical profession in general. Go to them for a simple headache, and all you get is off-the-cuff psychology, an old-fashioned lecture and pills that don't work, she muttered to herself.

Felicity let the newspaper slip to the floor, and decided to call Miles and Sherri. As forest rangers, they were hard people to reach; her mother had cautioned her to try every night to ensure success.

"We don't want to miss the baby's arrival," Emily Barrett had emphasized. "At least give Miles your hotel phone number so he can get in touch with you."

The plans called for Felicity to travel to the hospital when Sherri went into labor, then go back to the ranger station to help with the new baby. Sherri's due date wasn't for a few more weeks, though.

Felicity picked up the phone and dialed, remembering how her mother hoped Sherri would have a girl. Roger, who had married early, had two sons, and Emily's heart was set on having a granddaughter.

"I'm sorry. Your call did not go through as dialed," came the familiar recorded message. "Please check the—" Felicity hung up, disappointed. The phone connection to the remote ranger station was unreliable at best. She would have to try again later.

In desperation she once again picked up her stack of newly purchased reading material. She'd never been able to relax easily, and when she wasn't working she quickly became edgy. Her headache increased after five minutes of reading one of her business journals, and she disgustedly tossed it aside. With a grimace of distaste, she also passed over the cowboy book. No, the Western, she remembered, mentally correcting herself.

That left only the small book on the history of Silverton. Fortunately the print was large and clear; maybe she could manage to read without aggravating her headache. Curiously she scanned the inside blurbs, eager to see what else she could learn about the author.

There was a recent picture of Seth, with the engaging smile that had drawn Felicity to choose him as her pretend saloon-girl customer. The biography said he'd been born and raised in Silverton, and was an only child. He had attended school at the University of Colorado in

Boulder. There he had received a degree in American history, with a minor in mineralogy. Although his parents had retired to Florida to get away from the rugged winters, Seth had remained in Colorado to pursue a higher degree and a career as an historian and technical consultant. He was thirty-two, single, and welcomed any queries regarding state history.

Felicity nodded to herself. No wonder Seth had been irritated when he found she'd taken a job here. He could probably have used the salary himself. He couldn't earn all that much as an historian and consultant. Still, Flo had said he was good at his job, so he must manage to make some kind of living. It couldn't cost much to live in this little town, anyway.

Felicity reached for the second pillow on the double bed, and placed it on top of the one she was using. Propped up, she opened the book to the first page and began to read. An hour later she was still reading, her headache forgotten as she immersed herself in the fascinating history of Silverton.

In 1860 huge deposits of silver were discovered, and the remote and rugged land was never the same again. Thousands of workers arrived to work the mines. During Silverton's boom-town days, more than five thousand miners crowded the saloons and hotels on Blair Street. In the next thirty years, over four hundred million dollars worth of silver was taken from the earth. Then came the silver crash of 1893, and the great exodus began. Saloons, dance halls and miners' shacks were all boarded up and abandoned to the fury of the winter storms.

Silverton could have ended up as just another of the numerous Rocky Mountain ghost towns, save for one fortunate twist of fate. The Durango and Silverton Railroad, better known as the D&S, which had been established specifically to take the miners to Silverton and transport the silver ore to the southern town of Durango, was the town's salvation.

The train kept running, the serious-faced miners were replaced by awestruck tourists, and Silverton remained alive, thanks to its greatest natural resource, the majestic mountains.

Felicity finally came to the last chapter, which listed the remaining active gold and silver mines. Excluding the merchants, most of the other residents still earned their living in the mining industry. When she finished the final page, Felicity was disappointed that there was nothing left to read. Seth Tyler had made the past come alive.

And if she was honest, she'd have to admit he'd made her come alive today, too. She remembered how under his gaze she'd thought of herself as Felicity Barrett, woman, instead of Felicity Barrett, businesswoman, for the first time in ages. And it had nothing to do with that ridiculous saloon-girl outfit, either. It had to do with his attitude toward her, the interest she saw in his eyes—and with the totally womanly way she had responded to that interest. She'd enjoyed being with him, and she thought that maybe he'd felt the same. Until he found out that she was taking a job away from a local.

If only Seth hadn't disapproved so bitterly of her working in the commercials. She hadn't known him long, but after reading his book, she thought she knew at least a little about him. And she felt an irresistible urge to find out more. She slowly closed the book and placed it beside the end table's old-fashioned lamp.

Maybe if she talked to Seth again, she could set things right. But how should she proceed? She was used to men doing all the pursuing. She rarely exerted herself over anyone. She just wasn't interested. And here in Silverton she certainly wasn't looking for a vacation romance, she told herself. But that didn't make her feel any better about Seth's desertion.

She could ask him to autograph his book tomorrow, she thought with satisfaction as she changed for bed. That would be a good excuse to talk to him. She turned off the light, stretched out under the down quilt, and closed her eyes, falling asleep easily for the first time in more than a year.

EARLY THE NEXT MORNING Felicity was back on the job, costumed, this time, in a more modest calico dress and bonnet. As usual, her part was minor. The purpose of this particular commercial was to film the daily gunfight battle that took place on Blair Street during the 1870s and '80s. The stuntmen, several of them locals, had already been recruited, and the filming had gone smoothly. Felicity's part required her to run for cover inside the feed store once the shooting started.

"All right, people, listen up," Bill announced. "I don't want any mistakes today. We're behind schedule, and we still have yesterday's commercial to reshoot. Watch your cues, and all of you extras and walk-ons, *please* try to act professionally."

Bill stared straight at Felicity, who blushed and looked elsewhere. She had every intention of asking Bill to find someone else to take her place before they refilmed yesterday's commercial. There was no way she was getting back into that saloon-girl costume unless they found one that fit better, with the black boots Seth had insisted on.

If she could just get through this take without any mistakes, she would be free to talk to Seth. Felicity had spotted him beside Bill on several occasions, but hadn't been able to catch his eye. He seemed to avoid looking in her direction—or had she just imagined that? After all, the street was crowded, with a good-size gathering of actors and technicians standing around, along with some tourists who had stopped to watch the proceedings.

"Okay, everybody. Take your places. Ready? Action!"

Like the other extras, Felicity began her stroll up the pine sidewalks, trying to be an inconspicuous part of the scene. Even though she wore boots today, she chose her footing carefully, taking care to avoid repeating yesterday's disaster.

Suddenly two evil-looking riders galloped up the street, the horses' hoofs scattering dust. Felicity and the other extras looked up in feigned surprise. In the old days, no one ran their horses in or out of town unless something serious had happened. Even the Indians abided by that practice. Running horses meant excitement, and in her role as passerby, Felicity stopped to see what was going on.

The sheriff and his deputy came out of the old jail, both looking grim. Felicity had met these two men before. Brothers Jim and Jesse Colt were part of the regular local stunt group who performed daily gunfights for tourists: ordinarily they were friendly and good-natured. The transformation from smiling coworkers to threatening men of law and order was quite impressive, and Felicity admired their acting skills.

"I heard you hung my pa, Sheriff," one of the outlaws yelled from horseback. "I've come to avenge his death."

Jim, the older and larger of the brothers, was playing the sheriff, and he slowly reached for his gun. "He killed and robbed three miners, Mister. He didn't leave me much choice. Now get off your horse and let me have your guns.''

The outlaw's answer was to pull his gun and fire a wild shot at the sheriff. Felicity screamed on cue, then dashed into the feed store. Once inside, her part was over. She hurried to the window where she could enjoy watching the rest of the mock gunfight.

By now the two outlaws had jumped off their horses, while Jim and Jesse, as the sheriff and his deputy, ran for cover. Guns were blazing, other bystanders were running for safety, and everything was proceeding as planned.

Bill gave a signal, cuing a third, previously hidden outlaw to start firing blanks from the roof of the feed store. Jim whirled around and took careful aim, while the outlaw above readied himself for his sudden "death" and his fall onto the mattress concealed in an open wagon below.

Jim fired, and as planned the man on the roof grabbed his chest. Slowly, dramatically, he started his roll down the gentle slope of the roof, to the flat portion that covered the pine sidewalk, and then onto the buckboard's mattress.

But the drama of his roll and drop onto the wagon was completely obscured by a riot of color. A hailstorm of tennis balls, in the fluorescent orange, yellow and green used by beginners, showered the roof and the street.

"What the—" Bill screamed, seeing the "dead" outlaw sit up in surprise as ball after ball rained down around him.

Without thinking, Felicity ran out into the street to get a better look. So did everyone else, but their unplanned appearance made no difference to Bill.

"Cut!" he yelled in fury. He and everyone else knew that this take was ruined.

Bill continued screaming, his assistants scurried around, and Felicity and the rest of the extras didn't quite know what to do. There was a frantic search for the perpetrators of the hoax, but no one was found. The old building had outside stairs leading to the second story, and anyone could have climbed the opposite side of the roof. A quick release of the tennis balls, an easy slide down to the flat portion of the roof above the sidewalk, and a short jump to the street would mean an uncomplicated escape for any fairly active person.

Finally Bill dismissed everyone for an hour while he determined how to proceed. Felicity immediately decided to search for Seth. As intriguing as the tennis-ball prank had been, there wasn't much she could do about it, though there *was* a chance she could set things straight with Seth.

Much to her dismay, the changing room where she'd left Seth's book on Silverton was still locked. Felicity looked around for the wardrobe mistress who had the key, but couldn't find her in the understandable confusion. Felicity was irritated at the disruption of her plan, but determinedly set out to find Seth, anyway. She would simply ask him if he'd sign the book later.

She hurried down the stairs of the wardrobe building, and as she rounded the corner onto the pine sidewalk, bumped right into the one person she was seeking. Seth reached for her arm to steady her.

"I seem to be making a habit of this, Miss Barrett."

His tone wasn't friendly, and Felicity couldn't help feeling disheartened. "I thought we were on a first-name basis."

"Not anymore," he said coldly as he released her, then started to leave.

Felicity grabbed his arm. "Wait! Are you in a hurry?" she asked.

Seth glanced at his arm, then at her with unmistakable meaning, and Felicity let go.

"I'm sorry," she said, pushing the huge calico bonnet off her head and down her back. "I just wanted to ask if you'd autograph my copy of your book on Silverton's history. I read it last night—and I really enjoyed it. It was excellent."

"I don't have time for autographing right now." Seth looked past her and down the street, his attention elsewhere.

"I'm sorry to have bothered you," Felicity said stiffly, hurt at his dismissal of her sincere praise.

"Perhaps later?" he suggested, still visibly anxious to leave. "I wanted to see if anyone found out who dropped the tennis balls."

Felicity stifled her feelings of exasperation and regret. "I wouldn't want to keep you from your technical consulting."

But then, because her feelings had been bruised, she was stung into saying, "By the way, you're falling down on the job. The next time you see those two old trainers who are handling the dogs for these commercials, tell them that Old West dogs didn't have flea collars or rabies tags. An expert like you should know that."

Felicity turned to walk away, but not before she saw the stunned look that crossed Seth's face. This time it was his turn to grab her arm and stop her retreat.

"What did you say?" he demanded.

Felicity treated him to the same cold stare he had given her when she'd grabbed at him, but her arm remained firmly in his grip. "I already told you. Now let me go. You said you were pressed for time, and you've made your opinion regarding my presence quite clear."

With an obvious effort, Seth smoothed the anger from his face. He loosened his hold on her arm, but didn't let go. "I was in a rush because I wanted to check out the tennis-ball fiasco. You had a much closer view of the action than I did. I don't suppose you saw anyone suspicious?"

"No, not at all," Felicity answered, feeling a little better. Perhaps Seth *had* been rushing to see Bill, and not rushing to get away from her. "All I saw was the tennis balls. Someone must have been on the roof, but I didn't see who."

Seth's brow furrowed, then he slowly exhaled. "I suppose one less person at the scene of the crime wouldn't matter. There probably isn't much I could do anyway." His hurried manner faded away, and he now acted as though he had all the time in the world.

"If you still want me to autograph your book, I will," he said pleasantly. "Bill gave everyone an hour off."

"I don't have it with me. It's locked in the wardrobe room," Felicity explained.

"Then may I buy you a cup of coffee? Tea? A saloon-girl special?"

"What's that?" Felicity asked curiously, and Seth pressed his advantage by gently steering her down the street toward a little shop.

"Actually there's no such thing," Seth admitted. "I just made it up. But can I buy you a drink, anyway?"

Once again she felt Seth's magnetism, and despite a few vague misgivings Felicity let herself be convinced. The coffee-shop patrons and staff greeted Seth with the same easy familiarity she'd observed in Flo's drugstore.

They were quickly shown to a table. Felicity noticed that more than a few people casually watched her.

"It looks as if there aren't many nonresident customers here," she said, feeling slightly uncomfortable with the stares.

"Not too many in calico dresses and bonnets, either," Seth agreed.

"What'll it be, Seth?" asked the waitress.

Seth looked at Felicity. "I'd like some ice tea, please."

"Make mine coffee." Seth handed the waitress the menu, then gave Felicity his undivided attention. "How are the commercials going for you?"

"Better than yesterday. At least I've remained on my feet." *With my clothes in place,* Felicity silently added.

The twinkle in Seth's eye told her that he'd thought the same thing, but all he said was, "I'm glad Bill decided to take my suggestion about the boots."

"So am I."

The drinks arrived, and Felicity sipped hers gratefully. "Seth, I really enjoyed your book. Since I've read it, I can understand why you were so upset at my having this job. I'd still like to give you my checks so you can donate them to the town."

Seth shook his head. "There are some worthwhile charitable organizations around, but you're under no obligation. I'm sorry I overreacted. You applied for the position, and you were awarded it. Even though I'd still rather see the income go to a local person, you're entitled to the pay."

"Then it's too bad I'm not a local person," Felicity said lightly. "I imagine I'd fit in better if I wasn't a city girl."

"Sometimes even the local women don't fit in so well here." A shadow flitted across Seth's face, then he shrugged and changed the subject. "Tell me again about these technical errors I should be aware of," he coaxed. "I don't want to be accused of not doing my job."

Felicity poked her straw at the slice of lemon floating in her drink. "There isn't much to tell. I went to change clothes yesterday, and these two old men with four huge dogs were blocking the stairs in the alley. I asked them what they were doing, and one of them said they were handling the dogs for the commercials."

Seth's lips compressed into an unsmiling line. "And then?"

"I told them Bill had said there wouldn't be any more shooting for the day, so they might as well go home."

Felicity noticed Seth's fingers tightening on the handle of his cup.

"I don't suppose you got a really good look at them, did you?"

"Not really. I was too busy staring at the dogs. I do remember that both of the men were old, at least in their seventies. One of them was bald, and the other had very white hair. But I honestly don't know if I could pick them out of a crowd if I saw them again. Only... I don't think they really were with the film crew. They looked too..." Felicity frowned as she groped for the right words. "I don't know... out of place. And the dogs wore collars with tags. Real movie dogs wouldn't have had those, and wouldn't have needed leashes, either. They would have stayed in place by command alone."

"And you said you weren't with the film business." Seth's words were clipped, and Felicity had the feeling that her answer hadn't pleased him.

"I'm not, but that doesn't mean I'm blind." She put down her straw. "Between those dogs yesterday, and the crazy tennis balls today, I've decided that a life in show business can be quite bizarre.''

Seth seemed deep in thought; for some moments, he said nothing, but Felicity's next words jolted him out of his silence.

"You don't think the two incidents are related, do you?''

"Definitely not," he answered vehemently. "The old men you saw were probably just curious spectators. And I'm sure the tennis balls were just a prank pulled by some local kids. I wouldn't give either incident another thought.''

He signaled for the check. "I guess you have to get back to work," he said as he paid the bill, then left a generous tip. "Do you think you can find your way without me? It isn't far.''

Felicity checked her watch and saw that she still had plenty of time before the end of her break. It almost seemed as if Seth was trying to get rid of her.

"No problem," she replied, hiding her disappointment. "Thank you for the drink." Heavens, she *had* been hiding in her office too long if she couldn't hold a man's interest beyond the time it took to drink a glass of ice tea.

"I'll see you later, then.''

She stood and gathered up her long skirts. Seth helped her with her chair, then she was left to walk out of the coffee shop alone, feeling slightly let down. As she lifted the calico dress to step outside, she remembered that she still hadn't made any definite arrangements for Seth to autograph her book. She turned around, only to catch Seth watching her departure, eyes narrowed and his mouth a grim line. Felicity gave him a hesitant wave, then decided not to stop.

Seth certainly wasn't the type of man she was used to dating, Felicity thought as she trudged back to the shooting location. The business professionals who were her casual social companions might be dull, but at least she knew where she stood with them. She couldn't say the same about a man like Seth Tyler.

CHAPTER THREE

FELICITY PICKED UP her trade magazines and absently flipped through them. She was back at her hotel, having spent the afternoon as both the saloon girl, with sensible boots this time, and the calico-clad bystander. Bill had finally finished filming both commercials, free of any major incidents such as raining tennis balls or falling walk-on actresses. The finished version of the sheriff's gunfight commercial was far from perfect, but in view of how far behind schedule they were, Bill had decided to call it a wrap.

With a collective sigh of relief, Felicity and the rest of the cast had headed for home. Already the mountains were casting their long shadows against the town, and everyone was hungry and tired. And in Felicity's case, restless.

It was too late to go sight-seeing, and Seth had disappeared from the set before she'd had a chance to speak with him again. He'd been busy behind the cameras all afternoon; any attempts by a frustrated Felicity to catch his eye had been in vain. She could only hope his remoteness was work-related and not deliberate.

Felicity had once again tried to put a phone call through to her brother Miles. She was unsuccessful, and with time weighing heavily on her hands, she'd picked up her magazines.

After five minutes' reading, her temples started to twinge with the warning signals of another headache, and in disgust Felicity threw her magazine to the floor. Vacations were highly overrated, she decided, especially when you had no one to share them with. She might as well be back in her office in Portland with her spread sheets and business accounts. At least then the time wouldn't pass so slowly.

Felicity looked at her watch and decided against any dinner right now. She'd eat later, when the evening crowd was gone and a woman could sit alone without being bothered by overfriendly men.

Ashamed of her temper, Felicity rose from her chair and picked up the magazine. She guiltily smoothed the crumpled pages, then placed it back with her other reading material.

The glossy cover of the paperback Flo had insisted she have caught her attention. Felicity reached for it, then rolled her eyes upward in dismay. She, Felicity Barrett, sensible, intelligent businesswoman, was going to read a cowboy book. If anyone had told her she'd be spending her vacation reading frivolous stories about old-fashioned macho men and helpless fainting women, she would have laughed herself silly.

"I can't do it," Felicity said aloud. "This is ridiculous."

She reached for the phone again and tried one more time to reach Miles. Maybe Sherri had already given birth. A quick phone call to Bill, and then another for a helicopter, and she could be gone in the next hour. At least with the new baby, she could keep occupied, even if it did mean saying goodbye to Seth, she thought with sudden reluctance.

The telephone line was busy. Felicity drummed her fingernails on the end table, looked furtively around her, then picked up the Western and opened it to the first chapter. Anything had to be better than just sitting here alone. Settling down, she started to read. She'd made good progress into a surprisingly interesting opening when a knock on the door startled her.

"Just a minute," she called out, quickly closing the book over her finger before hurrying to the door.

It was Seth. "Good evening. Am I interrupting anything?"

"Uh, not at all." Felicity hid the book behind her back, careful not to lose her place. "Come on in."

"I came to autograph your history of Silverton, and to take you to dinner." He noticed the book in her hand as she closed the door. "What are you reading?"

"Just the book Flo wanted me to have," she reluctantly admitted. "Please have a seat." She gestured toward the one chair in the room, then turned down the corner of the page to mark her place. She exchanged the Western for the Silverton history.

"I thought you didn't read Westerns." Seth grinned, enjoying her discomfort at being caught.

"I don't." Felicity handed him a pen and the history book. "But reading the paperback doesn't bother my head too much. I've been prone to headaches lately," she explained matter-of-factly, with no self-pity. "My job's very demanding."

"Then you need a new job," Seth told her as he signed his name and returned the book to her.

Felicity shrugged as she sat down on the bed. "I like the one I have, but I do need to slow down. I'm an incurable workaholic, and I get bored stiff if I'm not busy.

I was forced on this vacation by my well-meaning but worthless family doctor."

"Ah." Seth exhaled with sudden comprehension. "And that's why you took the job as a walk-on? To keep busy?"

"I'm afraid so," Felicity admitted with chagrin. "At least the commercials give me something to do during the day. In the evenings I like to catch up on business reading, but I've had to forget about that for a while."

Felicity paused. She was glad to see him and reluctant to send him away, but she didn't know exactly where she stood with him. She'd better not press her luck.

"Anyway, thank you for the autograph." Felicity gave him an easy opening to leave, hoping he wouldn't take it. Vacations in a strange town could be very lonely, she'd learned, but she didn't feel lonely when he was around. The realization came as a surprise.

"You're welcome." Seth didn't seem to be in any hurry to take her cue, much to Felicity's delight. "Now, how about dinner? You haven't eaten, have you?" Seth asked.

"Not yet."

"Then let's go."

"We aren't going anyplace fancy, are we?" she asked, glancing down at her jeans and sweater.

"Oh, no. I thought I'd take you to The Bent Elbow. It has a buffet, and it's casual. But the food's great, and the place has an interesting history. It used to be the Tremont Saloon & Sporting House and was run by a woman named Big Tilly. Every would-be saloon actress should go there."

"Even mere walk-ons?" Felicity smiled, reaching for her purse.

"Especially those," Seth replied.

The Bent Elbow was crowded. It seemed to be a popular place with tourists, but Seth and Felicity didn't have to wait long for a table.

"I always imagine business executives as gray-haired men with pin-striped suits and snooty secretaries," Seth said once they'd been served. "You don't look like the high-powered executive type." His gaze slowly traveled down her figure, then back up to her face.

"Oh, but I am," Felicity admitted. "You should see my pin-striped suits back home. And I have two secretaries, though only one of them is snooty. You're looking at the heir apparent to Barrett Shipping in Portland, Oregon."

Seth sat up straight with surprise. "I've heard of it. It's a big company."

"Very big."

"So your headaches aren't from the high altitude?" Seth surmised.

"I'm afraid I brought them with me when I came," Felicity admitted ruefully. "What with our business growth and all, I sometimes don't know whether I'm coming or going. But I like it that way," she insisted.

Seth was not convinced. "You're much too young to be suffering from headaches and enforced vacations for executive burnout. Why don't you quit?"

"Quit?" Felicity echoed in astonishment. She had toyed with the idea now and again, but she'd never seriously considered it. Her father would regard her as another failure in the family business, as he did Miles. Besides, she liked her job.

"What else would I do with myself?" Felicity wondered. "If I'd wanted to be a lady of leisure, I could have become one years ago."

"You could travel, or find a new job, or pursue a new interest, or go back to school... The possibilities are endless."

"I don't know," Felicity said, uneasy with the new tack the conversation had taken. "Portland is my home. I wouldn't have left at all if my parents hadn't forced me to come here. I'm actually taking over my mother's vacation, you see. My sister-in-law lives in Colorado, and she's due any time now with her first child. Mom had planned on relaxing here in Silverton while waiting for the baby to arrive. So now I'm the one waiting for the baby instead."

"Your brother doesn't work for the company?" Seth asked curiously.

"Miles? Oh, no. He left home a long time ago. My brother hated Barrett Shipping, much to Father's disappointment. I have another brother at home, but Roger prefers to command the fleet. I'm the only one in the family trained in the administrative end of the business. I work in the marketing and sales department."

"Still, you could quit if you wanted couldn't you?" Seth persisted. "Surely your father could train someone else to replace you."

"Yes... I suppose he could, if I asked him." She shifted in her seat. "But the business needs me. And I like working. Believe it or not, I really do enjoy my job."

Seth studied her carefully, and she knew he'd noticed the faint shadows under her eyes. "Having a career doesn't mean working yourself into a state of exhaustion. For your own good, sooner or later you're going to have to learn how to relax."

Felicity smiled. "That might be harder than you think. I don't live in a town that's only open during the summer."

"What better place to learn than in Silverton? Stay here for the winter," Seth suggested. "When the tourists leave, we all go back to our own pursuits. I write, others practise their crafts and replenish the shops. Still others tend their livestock. And of course the mines are always being worked. We all live at our own pace. I think you'd enjoy it here, Felicity."

"It's a novel idea, Seth. But despite the fantastic scenery, I really don't think it's for me," she slowly replied. "It's different for you. You seem to know everyone in town—you grew up here. I'd have no one."

"You know me," Seth contradicted. "And look how many people you've met already."

"That's true. But I certainly couldn't find any work. And I wouldn't have much family nearby. I'd miss that. What about you, Seth? I read your bio in the book. You're single. You don't have any brothers or sisters, and your parents are gone. Don't you miss having family around? Don't you get lonely?"

Seth's expression lost some of its animation. He took a long swallow of his drink before he answered. "I was married."

"Married?" Felicity echoed. His book said he was single, and she experienced a moment's panic.

"Valerie was a local woman. We grew up together. She was an only child, too, and her parents lived near mine, so it was inevitable that we were frequently thrown together. Not that I minded," Seth quickly added. "I loved her very much. But I sometimes wonder if Valerie didn't marry me because that's what everyone expected."

"Was it a happy marriage?" Felicity asked hesitantly.

"Unfortunately it was a very short marriage." Seth's face went carefully blank. "She died in a car crash, and that was the end of any happiness. She was only twenty-two.''

"Seth, I'm so sorry."

"Thank you. It was more than ten years ago, and I'm certainly over the worst of it, but sometimes I wonder what things would be like today if we hadn't married so young. My parents still feel bad about Valerie and me. They moved to Florida shortly after she died. Too many sad memories, I suppose."

Seth took another sip of his drink. "What about you? Why is an attractive woman like you still single?"

Felicity was too shaken by his story to enjoy his compliment, but she did her best to answer. "Being the boss's daughter is a definite disadvantage. The really scrupulous men avoid me like the plague because they don't want to be accused of dating me to further their careers. Not that I don't have dates," she hastened to explain, "but I haven't met anyone I've really been interested in. I tend to be either bored or suspicious. Financially, I *am* quite well-off," she said without boasting.

"There's been no one special at all?" Seth asked.

Felicity smiled ruefully at a sudden memory. "Well, there was this one man I really cared about. I was sure I'd finally met Mr. Perfect."

"And he wasn't?"

"Far from it. Quite by accident one day, I overhead him describing to his buddies how he planned to spend my money. One of those ways was keeping his present girlfriend as his mistress, since I really wasn't his type at all."

Seth's eyes flashed angrily at her words. "It must have been rough."

Felicity shrugged. "Like you, I'm over the worst of it now. I was just glad I found out before the wedding instead of after. I threw myself into my work again after firing Mr. Perfect and giving him the worst reference in Barrett Shipping's history,'' she added, the corners of her mouth curving upward.

Seth raised his glass. "Hear, hear."

"I'm much more skilled when it comes to business than romance," Felicity admitted. "But I'm always hopeful. I keep my options open."

"Maybe you just haven't met the right man," Seth replied lightly.

"Maybe not," Felicity replied just as easily, although inside, she was anything but composed. She was no stranger to harmless flirting, but with Seth it took on an exciting intensity.

"A shame," was all he said. "Would you like some dessert now?"

"No, thank you. I have to get up early tomorrow morning for work. I'd better call it a night."

Seth nodded. "I'll walk you back to your room," he said.

Once at her door, he unlocked it, then followed her in. Felicity threw her purse on her bed, and sat down, suddenly feeling the effects of a long day. Seth casually seated himself on the chair and leaned back, obviously in no hurry to leave.

"Are you sure you don't want dessert?" he said. "We could have the hotel send something up here."

"It's been lovely, Seth, but I'd better not. My head is still bothering me, and I really think I need to go to bed."

"I can take care of that headache for you." He left his chair for a spot next to her on the bed, and brought his hands up to her shoulders. "It's probably all tension. I've been told I give a great massage."

"Oh, really? By whom?" Felicity asked, her voice sharper than she'd intended.

Seth smiled at her question. "Why? Are you jealous?"

"Hardly," she said, trying to sound nonchalant. Why wasn't she her usual composed self on this date? Felicity felt his hands gently kneading her shoulders. She knew she should shake herself free and move to the now-vacant chair, and she *would*—but not just yet.

"My father ended up with a bad back from all those years as a carpenter. I used to do this for him every night before he could sleep. Only it was never this much fun."

Felicity started at that, but Seth's fingers held a sort of magic, and she felt her muscles begin to loosen again.

"Better?" he asked softly, his lips so close that his breath softly caressed the back of her neck.

"I didn't ask you to autograph my book with any ulterior motives in mind, Seth," Felicity managed to say. "That's not my style."

"I know." His hands continued their movements, sliding up to the tense area at the base of her skull. "And I didn't come with any ulterior motives, either, except to enjoy your company." His hands continued their ministrations. "And I must admit, I'm enjoying it very much," he said, his voice low and serious.

"Seth, I think you'd better stop." Felicity knew they both were enjoying more than just each other's company. The feel of his hands on her skin was exquisite, and she was afraid that if she waited much longer, she'd lose her resolve to send him home. Funny, she'd never had that problem with men before. Usually she couldn't wait to show them the door.

"You think so? Why?" Seth's voice was even softer now, promising her all manner of new delights. Felicity had no doubt this man could keep those promises—but then what?

"Just..." Felicity swallowed hard, and tried to ignore her body's tempting demands. "Just because. Perhaps you'd better leave."

Seth's hands gently turned her so that she was once again facing him. "I don't feel like calling it an evening yet."

He bent toward her and kissed her, his lips first gentle, then more intimate. Felicity couldn't help but respond, and when he finally pulled away, her mouth felt cold and bare.

"Again," he murmured, and Felicity knew her eyes were soft and inviting.

He pulled her close for another kiss, and this one was so tenderly intimate that Felicity finally came to her senses. "No more," she said firmly.

"Why not? Do small-town men pale in comparison to your big-city types?" Seth's eyes dared her to confirm his challenge, and Felicity hastened to reassure him.

"You don't bore me—just the opposite. In fact," she admitted, "I'm having a very hard time remaining sensible."

It seemed to Felicity that Seth received her words with something close to triumph.

"But..." She paused, pleasure at the sensations he had evoked mixed with genuine regret.

"But?" Seth prompted.

"I'm not going to be in Silverton long. Like I told you, once I hear that Sherri's had her baby, I'll be leaving. After that, I'm going back to Portland. I'm not the kind of person who settles for—" Felicity stopped, then plunged ahead "—a vacation massage." She spoke the words softly, to take away their sting. After all, they were both adults, and he might as well know how things stood.

"I didn't think you were. And for your information—" Seth's eyes took on a blazing intensity "—neither am I. I like to finish what I start. And you, Felicity Barrett, are unfinished business." Seth removed his hands and stood up.

Felicity was startled by his vehemence, and it was a moment before she regained her composure. She decided that now was the best time to rise from the bed and open her door. She was rapidly losing control of this conversation—and of herself, she realized. Her mind was already teasing her with what could have happened if she hadn't stopped him.

"Thank you for dinner, Seth. Good night." She noticed that her voice wasn't as firm as she would have liked.

Seth nodded. "I'll see you tomorrow, then, and let you get some sleep."

He was still alarmingly close, and Felicity felt her heartbeat quicken. A good-night kiss was no new experience for her, but this small-town man was setting off warning bells like no Portland man had ever done. While she was still debating whether to close the door after him, Seth took matters into his own hands.

He gave her a slow smile as his arms pulled her hard against his chest. He kissed her one final time with lips that tantalized, tasted and wantonly lingered over hers. Felicity felt herself sigh blissfully and then she felt him draw away.

"I won't keep you any longer," he said, his eyes alive with a blazing fire that didn't match his easy parting words.

"I—I . . ." Felicity stammered. It was only a kiss, she reminded herself. "Good night, Seth."

But Seth still didn't leave. "About your job making those commercials . . ."

"Yes?" Felicity's hands tensed. She hoped Seth wasn't going to drag out the subject of her taking work from a local again.

"Be careful on the set, okay?" His face was now deadly earnest.

Felicity experienced a strange feeling of unease. "Just what do you mean?"

"Just . . . watch yourself, all right? I've been trying to keep my eyes on things, and so far no one's been—" He broke off abruptly.

"No one's been what?"

Seth's expression instantly became closed and tight. "Fired. No one's been fired yet, and I intend to see it stays that way. Just be careful," he repeated. "Good night."

He wās gone. Felicity watched the door swing shut, and she sank back onto the bed with trembling limbs. Why would a man who had just kissed her with a thoroughness that set her body on fire suddenly warn her to be careful? And why did she get the feeling Seth hadn't told her everything?

Mysterious men weren't her type, she scolded herself. She had no intention of playing mouse to the secretive tiger that surfaced in Seth at the most inopportune times. Sensible women should seek out predictable men, she tried to convince herself.

And sensible city women should avoid small-town men who ominously warned outsiders to be careful at their jobs—especially small-town men who awakened exciting new sensations in those same city women.

Felicity's head was whirling with unanswered questions, and her body was crying with unanswered needs. She climbed into bed, determined to sleep, but found it impossible. Finally she decided to try her paperback again. She had left off reading where the hero had just met the heroine, a determined woman who was a match for him any day. It wasn't a trade journal, but the setting and background history were just as interesting, and so were the characters, Felicity had to admit.

If nothing else, the plot would provide her with a distraction from Seth Tyler, and as far as Felicity was concerned, that was justification enough for reading such frivolous material.

FELICITY YAWNED MIGHTILY, then groaned, ignoring the curious looks of the other women in the wardrobe building. Six in the morning was a terrible time for anyone to be at work. Six in the morning was also a terrible time for anyone who had stayed up until well after midnight finishing a paperback Western. That crazy book with the ridiculous cover had actually been a pretty good story.

Felicity had become caught up in it. The hero was a man whose own personal honor and "code of the Old West" clashed with the heroine's values. She was a woman who had been tragically wronged and wanted justice at any price. Eventually the happy ending had occurred, but the suspenseful path that led to it had surprised Felicity, who'd expected the usual clichés and predictable plot twists. Her late-night reading, along with dreams of Seth Tyler as the hero in the book and herself as the other woman the hero ignored, made for early-morning torture when her alarm rang.

Felicity yawned again. There was a lot to be said in defense of family businesses. Back home she could have come in late. She gulped her second cup of coffee before beginning the arduous task of buttoning up her black boots. Today she was dressed in the heavy blue brocade of a traveling costume. Bill was filming a commercial with one of Silverton's stagecoaches, and Felicity would be among the crowd of people waiting at the station.

Playing the part of a bored, sleepy traveler would be easy enough. The only thing keeping her awake was the cheerful realization that because this was a new commercial, Bill would certainly need Seth's help. Seth would definitely be on the set, and if she couldn't speak to him, at least she'd be able to see him.

Once she was outside, the crisp mountain air revived Felicity even more. She picked Seth out instantly. He seemed to be everywhere, darting in and around the crowds, talking with the locals and the film crew, and being greeted everywhere with a friendly word and a smile. Felicity wished she could talk to him, too, but it was her turn for makeup.

Much to Felicity's delight, some of the local people also greeted her by name. Her association with Seth had obviously given her some status among the locals. Jim and Jesse Colt took particular care to bring her juice and a cinnamon roll, and others made certain that she was never without company during the long periods between rehearsals.

Felicity continued to watch Seth, catching fleeting glimpses of him here and there. She noticed that she wasn't the only person who seemed drawn to him. More than one woman tried to catch Seth's eye, and that made her appreciate his wave and smile to her from across the crowd all the more.

"Aren't we ever going to get started?" Felicity asked Jesse Colt as the sun once again slipped behind the clouds.

Rehearsals were over, and the filming was due to start. The light had been bad all day, and now, right before lunch, it seemed worse than ever. Then the first drops of rain began to fall. Felicity hurried for shelter, knowing that her brocade costume would stain. Cameramen raced for their protective plastic tarps, and Bill was back on the megaphone.

"No one leave! I want to get at least one take of this commercial in today. The rain may let up in a few minutes."

"We're finished," Jesse told Felicity with his long-standing knowledge of the area's weather conditions.

"The rain's here to stay," Jim agreed.

Sure enough, a half hour later the rain was still falling as clouds settled in around the mountains. Most of the walk-on locals had confidently left to change and go home before Bill finally gave the official verdict. "That's it for today. Everyone should be back tomorrow morning at six, rain or shine." Then he was on his way indoors, too.

Felicity stayed under the shelter of the covered boardwalks and headed for the wardrobe building. She'd change and eat lunch, then take a much-needed nap. Perhaps later she'd go back to Flo's little drugstore and buy a couple more of Decker Townsend's Westerns. They were easy reading, she justified to herself, and didn't aggravate her headaches, which still appeared at the slightest provocation.

And there was something else in the book she'd read last night, something that whispered tantalizingly to her. Decker Townsend, through his hero and heroine, had described—no, promoted—the benefits of living in a small, isolated Western town. Felicity had never understood how anyone could be happy away from the many entertaining distractions of a large city. But the characters had seemed quite content, even enriched, by their isolation.

In a way, the book reminded her of the life her brother and his wife led in their remote ranger station. She had never comprehended how Miles and Sherri could be so happy in the middle of nowhere, with nothing but the barest of modern conveniences.

Felicity was curious to know if Townsend's theme of paradise in isolation just appeared in that one book, or if he'd used it in others, too. She intended to buy a few more of his stories to see. The sense of rural peace and simplicity the author had managed to convey gave her, for the first time, a glimmer of the way her brother and his wife must feel. Maybe she'd pick up those books before she ate lunch, she decided. There was something about them.... Perhaps they'd also explain why any place, even a dusty old town in a fictitious book, seemed preferable to living in her home city working at a job she loved.

Felicity reached the wardrobe building, changed, then hurried through the rain to Flo's drugstore, once again filled with a crowd of locals. The older men sitting outside on the covered porch waved and greeted Felicity by name as she approached the entrance.

"Seth's inside," one of them announced. "He's been looking for you."

"Really?" Pleasure overrode embarrassment as four pairs of kindly eyes all twinkled at her. It seemed that a man waiting for a woman in a drugstore had a far more romantic message in Silverton than it did in Portland.

"Yes, ma'am. He's one lucky guy."

Felicity felt the beginnings of a most uncharacteristic, unbusinesslike blush. Her hand flew to her hair. She was glad she had decided, while on vacation, to abandon her severe page-boy style for the gentle waves that brushed her shoulders. She hoped the rain hadn't ruined them.

"You look just fine," another of the white-haired men said, observing her totally feminine action. Felicity's hand froze, then she lowered it slowly.

At a loss for something to say, since Barrett Shipping certainly hadn't taught her what to do in situations like this, Felicity drew upon her dignity and swept by them, ignoring the good-natured laughter that followed.

"Hello, Felicity. I've been looking for you." Seth was leaning against Flo's counter, obviously waiting. "Isn't this great? We both have the afternoon off."

"She isn't going to agree with you, Seth," Flo warned. "You told me the lady doesn't know what to do with herself when she isn't working."

"I did not. Don't listen to her." Seth cheerfully jerked a thumb in Flo's direction. "Ever since my parents retired in Florida, she thinks she's entitled to information about my personal life."

"That isn't true!" Flo contradicted, though she didn't seem upset in the least. "He's made a few harmless comments about you, and I just repeated them."

"Do you discuss all your new friends with the drugstore staff, Seth?" Felicity wondered as she twirled the paperback carousel, looking for more Decker Townsend Westerns.

"Everyone knows a little talk of pretty women now and then is good for business," asserted a genial, heavyset man. "Right, Flo?"

Flo laughed, but Seth only smiled, and that smile was meant solely for Felicity. It was a heady feeling to know that she had his complete attention. It made Portland seem light-years away.

"And just what have you told them about me?" she asked, keeping her voice light, although her eyes shone with pleasure.

"Nothing much. A gentleman never tells," Seth answered.

Felicity was glad of that, for she suddenly remembered his hands gently kneading her shoulders in the hotel room, and the feel of his lips on hers. She tried to concentrate on the books instead.

"He only told us good things, miss," someone reassured her, and Felicity turned to see the four men from the porch now behind her.

"I didn't tell them a thing," Seth contradicted. "Some subjects I prefer to keep to myself."

It was obvious to Felicity that this good-natured banter was an old routine between Seth and his friends.

"Don't listen to those old fools," Seth said with a friendly look toward them. "Just because I consult with them once in a while on Silverton's history, they think they're entitled to be nosy. Especially Emil here. They don't know much, although they pretend to."

"Ha!" Emil, clearly the leader of the small group, snorted in mock derision. "We know your life history, and everyone else's in this town. If it wasn't for me and Walt and Mike and Vern here, your history of Silverton would read like an old high-school textbook."

Flo laughed. "He's got you there," she said.

"Ancient town history has nothing to do with Felicity," Seth replied, laying his hand on her shoulder. He was a very physical person, Felicity noticed, always touching his friends' shoulders, taking her arm, shaking someone's hand. There was nothing sexually suggestive in his touch, and all at once Felicity felt offended that there wasn't. That realization made her cheeks turn just the barest shade of pink.

Seth noticed. "Now you've embarrassed her. Felicity will think I have no taste when it comes to choosing my friends. I think you should all apologize."

Flo defiantly tossed her chin in the air, one of the men mumbled something unintelligible, and Emil gave her a bold wink.

Seth sighed with exaggerated long suffering. "Sorry, Felicity, but that's the best you're going to get from the lot of them."

Felicity quickly recovered her poise. "There's nothing to apologize for," she replied. Obviously these people were all Seth's friends. They meant her no harm. If nothing else, she was grateful to them. Their remarks showed that she had more of Seth's interest than she'd originally thought, especially considering his initial disapproval of her working in Silverton.

"I don't want to keep you from your friends, Seth. I only wanted to pick up something to read before I went to lunch."

"She's giving you the brush-off, Seth," one of the men teased.

"You're wrong, Walt," Emil answered back. "She's hinting for Seth to take her out to lunch."

"I am not," was Felicity's tart answer. "I only came here to buy a few more of Decker Townsend's cowboy books."

That drew a loud chorus of hoots and laughter from the men. "She does want lunch, Seth. Why else would the lady buy more of your Westerns?"

"What?" Felicity started, then stared at Seth. "*You're* Decker Townsend?" she said with disbelief.

"The one and only," Seth admitted.

"Now don't tell me you didn't know, Miss," Emil said.

"She didn't know, because I didn't tell her," Seth declared, but they all pretended to disbelieve him—or maybe they weren't pretending.

"Why didn't you tell me, Seth?"

Felicity still couldn't believe the news. Daniel Seth Tyler; Decker Townsend—the initials were the same. She remembered her fascination with Seth's historical account of Silverton, and mentally compared it to the Western she'd just read. Both books were written in an energetic, fast-paced style, and both shared a painstaking attention to accuracy.

"You didn't seem very interested in Westerns when we first met. I didn't see any point in bringing it up."

"Oh." Felicity quickly searched her memory and realized with relief that she hadn't said anything too harsh about Westerns. "But I read the one book Flo gave me, and I absolutely loved it! That's why I wanted to buy some more. I can't believe you're Decker Townsend. Why don't you use your own name for the Westerns?"

Seth eyes had lit up at her praise. "I know it's a ridiculous pen name, but my agent wanted me to use it, and I agreed. I keep the two identities separate. Seth Tyler's historical studies satisfy my first love when it comes to writing, and Decker Townsend's Westerns pay the bills. I enjoy writing fiction, but keeping my standing as an Old West historical expert has its advantages when it comes to getting work, so I prefer to push my alter ego into the background."

"But why don't you write history all the time, if that's what you love?" Felicity wondered.

"Like I said, history books don't pay the bills. And even if they did...well, I don't want to write history texts for schools and universities. I'm sure I could find ready buyers for my work, if that was the case. But I don't like the format. I don't want to present just a collection of dull, dry facts. What I really want to do is make actual people and historical events come alive."

"Fictionalized accounts of real events?"

Seth nodded. "Yes, with books that would bring these characters to life, all accurately within the perimeters of their existing, documented history."

"But?" Felicity prompted.

Seth lightly took her arm and moved her away from the cash register, since they were blocking other customers.

"Well, it's been done before, with stories based on Calamity Jane, Wild Bill Hickok and Jesse James. And there've been a few movies based on actual events, such as the Shootout at the OK Corral, or the Fall of the Alamo. But these are rare examples, and the books and screenplays often blatantly ignore documented history for sensationalism. There just doesn't seem to be a market for any other treatment."

Felicity understood. Her job had made her familiar with marketing problems, and she knew that no matter how good a product was, if you couldn't find a buyer, you were out of business. "And so...Decker Townsend's Westerns?"

"I still write both types of books, but there aren't any buyers for my manuscripts based on real people and events. My fictional books are the only things that sell, and I do try to work in as much historical data as possible."

"It seems a shame. I really enjoyed your book on Silverton."

"Even that book almost didn't get published. The town printed them because I'm a resident, and because they sell to tourists."

"I'd buy your historical books," Felicity asserted. "In the meantime, I'll settle for more of your Westerns."

"There's no need to buy any. I can provide you with copies."

"Hey, Seth, why don't you show her your private collection?" Emil interrupted.

"Yeah, Seth, by candlelight," Walt added, his eyes twinkling.

Seth smiled, then turned toward Felicity to include her in the merriment, but Felicity was frowning. Something was tugging at her subconscious. The two men who had just spoken seemed very familiar. She knew she hadn't seen Emil before, or Walt, who was equally outspoken. But the other two, Mike and Vern, the quieter ones— she'd seen them somewhere.

Seth noticed Felicity's frown and misinterpreted it. "Come on, guys, the lady doesn't appreciate your sense of humor. Let's go, Felicity. We'll get lunch someplace."

Felicity didn't move, but pointed at Mike and Vern. "Excuse me, weren't you two the men I saw with those dogs the other day?"

Everyone froze.

"I don't know what you're talking about, ma'am," Vern said politely.

"No, I'm positive I'm right. It was after the saloon commercial. I went to change my costume, and you were in the alley with those huge dogs. I told you Bill had canceled the shooting, so you weren't needed. Don't you remember?"

Both men's faces were suddenly blank, all earlier traces of friendliness gone. Felicity grew confused. "I know it was you. I even told Seth about it, because your dogs had tags and collars, and that wasn't authentic. Remember, Seth?"

Seth said nothing, but his hand on her arm suddenly tightened, and his eyes glittered dangerously.

"Seth, I don't understand. What's wrong?"

CHAPTER FOUR

"I THINK YOU'D BETTER BUY Felicity some lunch right now, Seth."

Flo's voice was harsh, even hostile, and Felicity looked at all of them in bewilderment. What had she said wrong? Obviously she'd made some dreadful faux pas, but she was at a loss to understand what.

Seth tugged at her arm and literally propelled her toward the exit. "Let's *go*, Felicity."

"I want to stay and find out what's going on! I'm not ready to leave!"

But it was useless. In a matter of seconds, Seth had her outside, off the porch, onto the dirt street and into the rain.

"I'm getting all wet. Seth, let go!" Felicity insisted, alarmed at the way he was gripping her arm.

"Get in, you're already soaked," Seth ordered as he opened the passenger side of a four-wheel-drive Jeep.

Obviously no one in Flo's drugstore had any intention of telling her what this was all about, Felicity thought. She'd have to find out from Seth. Besides, there was no sense in getting drenched when she could ride back to her hotel.

"Oh, all right," she said irritably, climbing in and crossing her arms on her chest. The rain was cold.

Seth got in, and started the Jeep. He turned the heater on high, then draped his waterproof jacket around her.

"Here, take this until the car warms up. You'll dry off soon." He backed up the Jeep and headed away from Flo's.

"I don't need your jacket, Seth. The hotel's only a few minutes away. What I'd really like is an explanation of what just happened back there."

"The explanation can wait. As for the jacket, I'd suggest you use it. It's a long ride to my place."

"Your place?" Felicity stared out the window through the heavy rain and the darkness of the afternoon. Sure enough, they were headed out of town.

"I don't recall asking for a change in destination, Seth. I don't know what you call this in Silverton, but in Portland we call it kidnapping." Her eyes flashed her disapproval.

"Tell it to the local sheriff. In fact, I can even give you his home phone number. He's a good friend of mine." His matter-of-fact tone told Felicity exactly how little help she could expect to receive from that end. "You might as well sit back and enjoy the ride."

"Great." Felicity exhaled angrily. She was miserable, wet and totally confused. "First you're Seth Tyler, then you're Decker Townsend. Who are you now? A caveman?" A large bump jolted the Jeep, and Felicity felt herself lose all contact with the seat.

Seth ignored her insult. "You'd better hurry with that seat belt," he calmly replied. "We're almost at a dried stream bed—it's a real roller-coaster ride."

Felicity studied him with dismay. He didn't seem to be joking, and she decided that a seat belt was an excellent idea.

"Do you drive this every day?" she complained as they hit another large bump, and the Jeep became airborne.

"Usually."

As the Jeep landed, Felicity grabbed the dash for support.

"Sometimes I walk. In winter, it's easier with a snowmobile, if you don't mind the cold."

"I think you're crazy!" Felicity closed her eyes as they approached a particularly large outcropping of granite. When she opened them, she saw that the Jeep had cleared it. "No wonder your parents retired to Florida. They probably couldn't stand the daily commute."

"My parents lived in town. I told you Dad was a carpenter. He liked to stay close to his work, though he did help me build my house."

"You didn't like living in town?" she asked after another teeth-rattling jolt.

"It was okay, but I wanted more privacy. Town would have been too crowded after I got married."

Felicity looked behind her, unable to see in the rain the small town with its eight hundred residents. Barrett Shipping employed more people than that. She supposed feeling crowded depended on what you were accustomed to, but that wasn't what held her curiosity.

"You built the house with Valerie in mind?" Felicity asked, feeling strangely unsettled at the news. She didn't know if she wanted to see where Seth's wife had lived, had left her mark.

"Actually I built it with children in mind. I always wanted children. But I didn't think my lack of them should prevent me from living there. Valerie never lived in the house, you know, so there aren't any ghosts around. She died before it was finished."

Felicity didn't dare pursue the subject, but she wondered if Seth still missed Valerie. After all, they'd grown up together. They'd probably been quite happy during their short marriage. No doubt Seth hoped that someday he would find someone else just like her—a hometown girl who loved the quiet life and would provide him with lots of children. Someone exactly the opposite of her. The thought stung, and Felicity winced as she felt the beginnings of another headache. She was quiet during the rest of the drive until Seth finally slowed the Jeep.

"Here we are."

Felicity unclasped her belt, straightened herself painfully and looked around. Despite the rain, she could see how the weathered gray wood of the expanded A-frame cabin gracefully blended in with the pines and surrounding rock formations. An open deck and large windows in front promised plenty of sunshine on bright days, while the stone chimney spoke of cozy warmth.

Seth drove under the wooden deck, a sort of overhang that seemed to double as a carport, and parked the Jeep. The deck also sheltered an outside staircase leading into the house.

"Come on in." He must have noticed her pale face, then, because he gently stroked her hair. "Another headache?"

"Yes," Felicity admitted as he took her hand to lead her up the stairs.

"I have some stuff in my medicine cabinet that will help." He opened the door and gestured her in.

The central room was warm, with plenty of places to sit, but Felicity continued to stand. Her jeans felt relatively dry, but her shoes and sweater were soaked.

"I'll get you some dry socks and another sweater," Seth said, turning on lights. Because of the dark clouds and rain, there was barely any illumination inside.

"Seth, I'm tired, and I want to go home. Just forget about the dry clothes. Say what you want to say so I can leave."

"And ruin my reputation as a good host? Stay put. I'll have you fixed up in a jiffy. You look terrible."

"Of course I do," Felicity muttered as he left the room. "I was up all night reading your cowboy book."

"That's Western," Seth corrected, not breaking stride.

Felicity could hear the amusement in his voice, and she rolled her eyes. Somehow, this wasn't exactly how she'd pictured her vacation.

"Feel better?" Seth asked half an hour later.

"Yes, I do," Felicity answered, her humor much improved. She was warm, fed and relaxed. Her headache had calmed considerably, and her skin basked in the comforting heat of the fire Seth had lit.

He added another log before taking a seat next to her on the couch. For a few moments nothing was heard but the crackle of burning wood and the steady beat of the rain on the pine deck outside.

"I'm still amazed you're Decker Townsend," Felicity said. "You could have told me."

"I gave you my reasons this afternoon. Besides, when a man's trying to impress a woman, the last thing he wants to do is bring up something that, uh, bores her."

Felicity smiled with pleasure. "Westerns don't bore me, Seth. At least, not yours. And I'd never read one before. I'm glad I found out you wrote them. If that old man, Emil, hadn't said—"

"About Emil and his friends..." Seth began. "I'm afraid you may have opened up Pandora's box."

"I know I did something wrong," Felicity said slowly, "but what? Why did everyone suddenly refuse to talk to me? And why did you drag me out of there like the store was on fire?"

"Felicity, there's a lot you aren't aware of. We've tried to keep it quiet, but there's been trouble between some of the residents and the film crew. Certain people in town resent the crew's presence." Seth paused. "The tennis balls were no childish prank. Their appearance was deliberately planned."

"But you told me yourself that the merchants need to make as much as they can during the summer. They must be doing quite well with the film crew here. And they'll do even better if tourism increases. Why would anyone want to jeopardize the money those commercials will bring in?"

"Most of us don't. No one has anything against the increased income. What's angering some of the townspeople is the . . . side effects of these commercials."

Felicity shifted impatiently. "I don't understand. The commercials mean more publicity, more tourists, and still more income. Isn't that what you want?"

"Theoretically, yes. But more tourists don't just mean more income. They also mean a change in our life-style. Felicity, you have to understand the way we live here. For nine months we live just like everyone else. Then summer comes and we're bombarded by trainloads of people. Our privacy is gone, and our homes and our businesses are suddenly open to the public. We're stared at, read about, photographed and commented on."

"I don't think I'd like that," Felicity said pensively. "You don't have any privacy at all."

"No, we don't. But most of us understand that it's necessary to our survival as a town. The old mines still being worked aren't going to last forever. The problem is with some of our older residents. They remember when Silverton was a regular town all year round. They don't like being a summer tourist haven, and they especially don't like the thought of an even greater number of tourists showing up next year. Most of these men worked hard in the mines all their lives, and they want peace and quiet for their declining years."

"And they're worried these commercials for the tourism department will make things worse?"

"I'm afraid so." Seth exhaled heavily. "Fortunately there aren't very many who feel that way, and I've been able to reason with most. But there remain a few troublemakers who pose a definite threat to the filming of the commercials."

"And they dropped the tennis balls?"

Seth nodded.

"Seth, I can't believe that a bunch of senior citizens would go climbing on roofs with a batch of tennis balls! Are you certain?"

"Yes, I am. They're good people, but they're somewhat...misguided." Before he could finish, Felicity had a flash of insight.

"Those two men from Flo's store! They're involved! They must have been the ones who tried to ruin the shootout scene! And they were going to release those dogs while Bill was filming the saloon fight commercial. Loose dogs would ruin the take, just like the tennis balls did. Am I right, Seth?" No wonder she'd received such a cold reception at the drugstore.

It seemed an eternity before Seth answered her. "Perhaps," he replied. "And if you *are* right, Felicity, what do you intend to do about it?"

"I..." She paused. "I don't know. If I was back in Portland, I'd call the police, report the pranksters and let them handle it."

"This isn't Portland, Felicity. This is Silverton."

Felicity didn't have a high opinion of lawbreakers, but she did have a high opinion of Seth. "You're the local,

I'm not. What would you do?" Felicity asked seriously, turning the problem over to him.

"Just what I'm doing now. I'm trying to reason with Emil. He's the leader, and he's more likely to listen to me than to some sheriff. I can't see getting him in trouble over a few tennis balls. Jesse and Jim Colt know what's going on, and so does Flo. Among the four of us, we think we can keep Emil and his friends under control."

Seth's face was expressionless, his voice casual, but the urgency in his eyes couldn't be restrained. "For now, I'd be grateful if you'd just let me handle this."

Felicity had been half-inclined to do that, anyway, but the expression in his eyes convinced her. "Well, no one's been hurt. I suppose a few loose dogs and a batch of tennis balls can hardly be considered dangerous."

"No, they can't." The insistence in his eyes disappeared. "And these men don't want to hurt anyone. They aren't criminals. They're just people who remember an earlier era—Silverton's good old days, so to speak. With luck, I can make them see sense."

"I just don't understand it, Seth. Why would anyone want to turn away business? There's so much potential for growth here, even if the town is isolated."

Seth shrugged. "That may be true, but most of us like things the way they are now, Felicity. Even I don't want Silverton to change. I just happen to understand the logistics of finance better than Emil and his gang. Three months of tourism is a small price to pay for our merchants' survival the rest of the year."

"I understand that, but how are you going to keep those pranksters out of trouble?" Felicity could still picture the two men waiting in the alley with their dogs. It wouldn't take much ingenuity to ruin future film takes.

"The less you know, the better," Seth said firmly. "Let me take care of this. I'm hoping to see the commercials finished without further incident. The last thing I need is for you to get involved."

"Why? Because I'm an outsider?"

"No, because I'm better equipped to deal with the situation than you are. These people are my friends. Besides, you're on vacation." Seth placed a calming arm around her shoulder. "You should be relaxing, having a good time."

Felicity let his arm remain where it was. "There's not much this vacationer can do when it's pouring rain," she observed.

His arm drew her close, as she had hoped it would, until their lips were only inches apart. "That's where you're wrong, Felicity. I can think of one thing."

He tightened his hold, and Felicity immediately knew what was about to happen. She didn't resist, but let his lips meet and take hers. Tiny coils of tension from the day's stresses unwound inside her, to be replaced by a feeling of wonder.

Seth slowly withdrew, his eyes soft as he studied her face.

"So how do you rate kissing city women?" Felicity asked, keeping her voice light. "Do you find us satisfactory?"

"Oh, yes," Seth murmured. "I've definitely decided to expand my horizons."

She felt his hand move from her neck to gently stroke her cheek, and her eyes closed as she savored the tenderness of his caress. He kissed her again, this time with more fire; more familiarity. His touch did things to her that had her skin shivering with pleasure, and she knew she was close to falling under his spell. But a small grain of common sense remained. When Seth went to kiss her a third time, she pulled away.

"What's wrong?" he asked, puzzled.

"I think we should stop for now."

Seth frowned. "Why?"

Felicity moved farther down the couch, leaving a safe distance between them. "I'm here on vacation. We both know I'll be leaving."

"What does that have to do with anything? You can't tell me there wasn't something between us a moment ago."

"It was very nice," Felicity said, trying to ignore the crying need Seth had awakened in her.

"Nice? It was more than *nice*, Felicity. Admit it."

Felicity did, but only to herself. "I told you once before, I'm not interested in casual affairs. You brought me here to explain about your friends, and now you have. There's no other reason for me to stay."

Seth's eyes narrowed, and Felicity was uneasy under his scrutiny. "Don't tell me you're afraid of a few kisses."

"I'm not afraid of kissing," she said tartly. "I'm just afraid of where it might lead."

Seth's eyes narrowed even more, but this time with satisfaction. "Really? Just how often do you have this fear of losing control?" he drawled.

"Never before," she blurted, "and I'm not sure I like it." When she saw the look on Seth's face, she realized exactly what she'd just admitted, and she bit her lip in embarrassment.

"I think you've been cooped up in your office a little too long—" Seth smiled "—or else those Portland men are pretty tame."

"Or maybe I'm just really tired," Felicity said, desperately trying to salvage her dignity.

"Then we'll have to try this again some other time when you're not so tired." Seth's eyes gleamed, and Felicity was excited and fearful at the same time.

"I think I should be getting back to my hotel," she said firmly.

"An opinion I don't agree with, but..." He stood up to get his car keys from the fireplace mantel. "We'll go, if that's what you really want. Is it, Felicity?" He studied her carefully.

Felicity started to lie, but suddenly she decided that Seth wasn't the kind of man to accept lies. She hadn't known him long, but somehow she trusted him enough to be honest.

"Seth, I don't want to go, not really. It's just that...Seth, you know I'm going to be leaving soon. I have my job and my family and my home and..." Shrugging, she raised her hands, at a loss for words.

Seth became very still, his hands frozen on the car keys. "What are you trying to say, Felicity?"

Felicity's hands went to her cheeks in confusion. "I'm getting spoiled...by your company, by your kindness." *By the touch of your lips on mine,* she added silently. "The more time I spend with you, the more I want!" she declared with surprising vehemence.

"Do you find anything wrong with that?" Seth asked, obviously pleased by her admission. "I don't."

Felicity dropped her hands into her lap and sighed. "No. I mean yes! I mean, it's all very nice, but it's going to be an awful wrench when I go home if we continue like this."

Seth dropped his hand from the mantel, the keys still in place, and turned around to face her. "*Nice* isn't exactly what I had in mind for us. But I must admit I'd be much happier if you were a local woman instead of someone half a country away.''

Felicity swallowed hard. "I'm no local girl, Seth. All the wishing in the world won't make it so.''

"No, I suppose not.'' It was Seth's turn to sigh now. He said nothing else, and Felicity's heart sank at the haste with which he had her back in his Jeep and on the way to town. She was miserable; he was silent and preoccupied. The ride home was agony.

To make matters worse, her headache had returned in full force, along with a sinking feeling that this innocent vacation acquaintance had suddenly bloomed into something far too important, something more likely to bring her heartbreak than happiness.

Back at the Grand Imperial, Seth escorted her to her room and unlocked the door.

"You'd better leave for home before it gets much later,'' Felicity said. "You have a rough drive back.''

"Felicity, I'm more worried about you than about how late it is, or when I get home.'' He took in her pale face. "You look terrible. Is your headache back again?''

Felicity nodded and sat down on the bed. "Yes, but I can take care of it.''

Seth ignored that. He picked up her prescription painkillers from the nightstand and read the label before shaking one of them into her hand. "These things would tranquilize an elephant. Stay put. I'll get you some water.''

Felicity felt perilously close to tears. "I can get my own water, Seth. I really wish you'd just go home.''

Seth's jaw clenched stubbornly. "Not until I know you're all right.'' He held out the water glass and she took it, careful not to touch his fingers with her own.

"I won't be all right until I'm back in Portland," Felicity replied.

"Thank you ever so much," Seth said in a tight voice. "You don't understand what's going on here at all, do you?" he asked harshly.

Felicity didn't say anything. She understood only too well what was going on inside herself. She was falling head over heels in love with Seth Tyler, and her only defense was a quick retreat to Portland. Before it was too late. If it wasn't already too late...

"Maybe it won't be so easy for me, either, when it's time for you to go," Seth said.

Don't say that, Seth, Felicity pleaded inwardly. *You're only making this harder.* "I'm not promising anything," she said aloud, her voice trembling.

"Neither am I, Felicity, because I don't believe in love at first sight. I don't think it exists. Love takes time. But it has to start somewhere, and if this is *our* somewhere, I'd be a fool to throw away my chance to find that out."

"That's just my point, Seth!" Felicity cried out. "We don't have that time! We don't! I'm leaving soon, and you're staying."

"Then we'll just have to make the best of whatever time we have, won't we?"

Felicity backed away at the warning in Seth's voice, but it was too late. The water glass was yanked from her hand and slammed down on the table, the pill skittered across the floor, and then Seth's arms were around her. His kiss and the range of emotions it expressed took Felicity by surprise. There was anger, and there was passion. And incredibly, there was also a deep longing, a desire for fulfillment that Felicity instantly recognized, for it mirrored her own.

This was not the sweet caress of earlier. This was a demand, a possessive, provocative kiss, unlike any Felicity had ever experienced, and she responded instinctively. She felt both excited and frightened by the intensity of his passion—and her own. She clung to him tightly, tipping back her head to better meet his embrace.

Just when she thought her unsteady legs couldn't possibly support her any longer, Seth released her. She collapsed onto the bed, waiting breathlessly for his next words. What would he say? What could *she* say to such passion from a man she had only recently met, yet felt she had known forever?

Seth pulled a small paper bag from his pocket and tossed it on the bed. "You forgot your books. Good night, Felicity."

Then he was gone. Felicity stared at Seth's Westerns with a feeling of unreality. Life back in Portland was never like this.

THE RAIN WAS GONE by the next morning, and at six o'clock Felicity was back at the wardrobe building, once again changing into her heavy blue brocade outfit. Bill was reshooting the stagecoach commercial that had been rained out the day before.

She hadn't seen Seth yet. As a consultant, he didn't need to appear early; he didn't need the attentions of costumer, hairdresser or makeup artist. Felicity wondered if he would be all business when he did arrive, or if she would see any trace of the blazing, passionate side of him she had witnessed last night.

After everything that had happened between them, it was hard to predict. In spite of her exhaustion, Felicity had again lain awake for several long hours. She felt guilty and distressed about how the evening had ended, suspecting that Seth considered her either a coward or a fool. Or both. And much as she wanted to explore her feelings for this man, she knew their situation was hopeless. Seth's devotion to his town came between them. How could he ever leave it? And there was nothing here for her—nothing except Seth.

Felicity knew better than to let him make love to her again. Those kisses... Even thinking about them was playing with fire. True, she had wanted to meet Seth almost from the first time she'd seen him, but she had no idea how quickly her yearning for him would grow, how urgent it would become. Why, oh why, couldn't she have met someone like him in Portland? And if she couldn't, then why did she have to meet Seth at all?

There was no future in this, she tried to convince herself. Seth wasn't about to write his books on Western history in Portland, of that Felicity was positive. Nor was he about to marry an outsider. After all, his first wife had been a local girl. No, it was hopeless. What would she do with herself if she did stay in Silverton? She could hardly work for a shipping business in the middle of the Rocky Mountains. Besides, she couldn't abandon her father. Frank Barrett had already lost Miles to Colorado. How would he take another defection by one of his children?

Lying in bed, Felicity had tried to force herself to be logical about the whole thing. She knew that most men didn't consider a kiss as serious a matter as most women did. She wouldn't deny herself the pleasure of his company, but she *would* try to keep their friendship at arm's length. Then, when Sherri had her baby, she would settle for a regretful but firm parting, and that would be that. Felicity pushed aside all thoughts of how painful that parting might be.

The doctor had said she needed her rest. She shouldn't be letting the problems of one small town and one bigger-than-life man keep her up nights. And that went for his books, too. Felicity hardened her heart and decided that she would not read any more of Seth's Westerns. She'd take them home for her nephews, but that was all.

Cowboy books and Old West historians simply weren't her style. The sooner she shed her jeans, Western paperbacks and foolish heart for her linen suits, trade journals and Barrett Shipping, the better off she'd be.

"Are you almost ready?" the wardrobe mistress asked, startling Felicity out of her reverie.

"Almost." She stood up, her boots all buttoned, and reached for the heavy jacket that went over the long-sleeved, lace blouse and the full, heavy skirt. Thank goodness the mountain air was cool. A woman could easily swelter in all this material, Felicity thought, as she started down the stairs to the dirt road.

"You!"

"Me?" Felicity said with surprise. Bill was waiting for her outside.

"Yes, you. You're taking the lead actress's part."

Her eyes opened wide. "Why? I'm not a regular actress."

"That may be, but you're the only woman who has a traveling costume. There's been a problem. Someone broke into the women's wardrobe building last night, and stole all the costumes for today."

"Stole them!" Felicity gasped. It seemed that Silverton's senior citizens had struck again. So much for Seth's efforts to keep the men in line. "Why was my costume left untouched?"

"There was a split seam, and the seamstress took it and a few children's costumes back to her hotel room for repairs. Thank goodness we have this one left," Bill said disgustedly. "It's a very small size, and you're the only woman we have who can fit into it."

Felicity looked at her costume, then back at Bill. "Surely you can find someone else to do this. I'm no actress."

"Sorry. We only have five regular actresses with us, and they're all much taller than you. I can't afford the time to alter the costume. You'll be the woman getting on the stagecoach and having the family reunion scene with your daughter and husband out at the old mines."

"But—"

"But nothing. We have no one else. These commercials have been nothing but trouble since the day we started," he grumbled. "I don't know what happened to all our costumes, but yours was left intact, so now *you're* the lead."

Bill yelled for the makeup artist and hairstylist, all the while leading a reluctant Felicity to the stagecoach station.

"For heaven's sake, get her a hat!" he ordered as they appeared and began fussing with her appearance.

"I don't have to talk, do I?" Felicity asked nervously.

"You certainly do." Bill thrust some papers into her hands. "Here's your lines. There aren't that many. Learn them."

Felicity stared at the script in horror. "But I'm just a walk-on!"

"Not anymore, Miss Barrett. You've been promoted. You signed a contract saying we could do that."

Felicity's mouth dropped open.

"Welcome to show biz, lady. Break a leg." With that, Bill strode off.

A half hour later Felicity was primped, primed and ready for her part. One of the local Silverton stagecoaches, along with its four-horse team, was preparing to drive into the station and discharge its passengers. Jim Colt, dressed as a miner, would stay inside the stage, and Felicity and the little girl would join him.

Jesse Colt, the driver, would then guide the stage to one of the old abandoned mines. There, Felicity and the little girl would have a mock reunion with their make-believe husband and father.

Felicity's hat, a stubborn, sliding piece of silk and feathers that refused to stay in place, was being pinned once again to her hair when Seth appeared.

"Hi, Seth!" the little girl called out.

"Hi, Denise. Felicity." He gave her a cool nod. "How's the next Shirley Temple?" Seth rumpled the child's hair, much to the hairdresser's dismay, and Felicity guessed that Denise was another local.

The child had only giggles for Seth.

"Since when do you two ladies rate your own hairdresser?" he asked Felicity curiously, watching the stylist repair the effects of his greeting to Denise.

"We're going on the stagecoach," Denise said, hopping excitedly from one foot to the other. "We get to be the stars!"

Seth's face froze. "Is this true, Felicity?" he demanded.

"Yes, and I'm not any happier about it than you are. Bill said that all the women's costumes for today were stolen. The seamstress happened to have our costumes with her, or they would have disappeared too. And I'd bet my paycheck on who took them," Felicity said, not concealing her irritation.

The white fury on Seth's face confirmed her guess. "They told me they wouldn't interfere anymore! I don't want you on that stagecoach, Felicity, and that goes for Denise, too."

Denise looked up in confusion and said, "But we're just going to ride in the stagecoach out to the old mines."

Seth's jaw hardened visibly. "Not if I have anything to say about it." He strode off in Bill's direction.

Denise tugged at Felicity's skirt, her little face worried. "What's wrong?" she asked.

"I don't know, but I intend to find out. You wait here," Felicity told her as she hurried after Seth.

Both Seth's and Bill's raised voices could be heard easily.

"This commercial isn't historically accurate! The stages didn't drive out to the mines in the 1860s, and you know it," Seth was saying.

"They do now, and we want the tourists to know that," Bill argued. "I'm not going to cancel this commercial!"

"I don't think you should be taking the stagecoach out to the mines, especially with untrained actresses in it."

Felicity nodded. She agreed with that one hundred percent.

"My *trained* actresses have no clothes! They were stolen!" Bill's voice grew louder and louder. "Everything that *could* go wrong in this little town of yours *has* gone wrong."

"Then why don't you wait for the regular actresses' costumes to turn up? With my help, it shouldn't take long," Seth insisted. "Denise and Felicity won't object, I'm sure."

Bill shook his head vigorously. "I have a schedule to keep. I'd like to save enough time to reshoot that gunfight scene, which means the stagecoach commercial gets shot *now*. Miss Barrett's contract says she has no choice, and the child's mother agreed to let her daughter ride in the stage. There isn't much that can go wrong, and that's the *end* of the subject.''

Seth was visibly angry as Bill stormed off, but Felicity finally dared to approach him.

''Seth, surely one historical inaccuracy isn't that important?''

Seth gave her a look of penetrating intensity. ''It isn't the historical inaccuracies I'm worried about.'' He hurried over to the stagecoach, and Felicity followed, her silk hat wobbling atop her head.

''Jesse, I want you to check out this stage from top to bottom,'' Seth ordered. ''Make sure that everything's in working order. And that goes for the horses, too.''

Jesse nodded, his face as grim as Seth's as he began his task.

''Jim, I want you to keep an eye on Denise and Felicity when the three of you are inside the coach,'' Seth said in an undertone. ''I don't want any more ruined takes, do you understand? And you and your brother be careful.''

''Seth, what is going on?'' Felicity demanded. She wouldn't admit it, but she was feeling more than a little nervous.

''I just want to make very certain that any pranks don't get out of control,'' was all Seth would say.

''If you think your friends are up to something, I want to know about it!'' Felicity was determined to press him for more information, but she was interrupted by Bill's megaphone.

''Ready?'' Bill's voice blared through the crowd. ''Everyone take your places. I want to get this right the first time.''

The stagecoach retreated to its starting position. Then Bill's assistant spoke into his walkie-talkie, signaling Jesse Colt to begin the approach into town. At the boarding station, Felicity anxiously reached for her hat one last time to make sure it was still in place. She quickly scanned the crowd, trying to find Seth. What was he so worried about?

"Okay, action!"

The cameras began as the stagecoach jangled and bumped its way into town. At the station, Felicity reached for her "daughter" Denise's hand, and began to play the part of a traveler. She chattered about the upcoming family reunion with the little girl, and although her words weren't exactly those in the script, she was close enough that Bill nodded with satisfaction. Denise was line-perfect; in fact, Felicity had to bite back a smile at the child's on-camera presence.

The stagecoach, a red painted and wood-toned duplicate of the original Western Concord model, pulled into town. Felicity waited for all the passengers except Jim to get off before she and Denise were helped aboard by stage-line workers. Felicity remembered just in time to hand them her mock passenger tickets.

She then settled Denise next to her on the leather seats, while the little girl, following her lines, chatted on about how pretty the matched set of four bay horses was. Felicity made what she hoped were the right responses, and stole a look at Jim. As he was supposed to be a stranger to her, they had no scripted dialogue, but she was reassured to see Jim keeping a close eye on both of them nonetheless.

The stagecoach quickly cleared the buildings at the edge of town, with the cameras on the film trucks keeping pace. Open meadows with their blue columbine, orange Indian paintbrush and yellow buttercups sped by, but women traveling a century ago would have stayed away from the dusty glassless windows, so Felicity tried to appear ladylike and uninterested in sight-seeing.

Still, she couldn't help but notice that many tourists and local people stood on the same side of the dirt road as the camera truck, though they were farther back and safely out of the way. They were all watching with interest, and Felicity found herself wondering if Seth was out there somewhere.

She adjusted her hat, which was starting to slip again with the bouncing motion of the stage. She mentally reviewed her lines for the mining-camp scene. Much to her surprise, the stage started to slow, and Felicity glanced out the window. The horses had reduced their fast trot to a walk, then stopped completely, nowhere near the old mines. Felicity's script said nothing about a stop, and she broke character immediately.

"Jim, why are we stopped? Has something gone wrong?"

Jim looked more puzzled than worried. "The horses usually stop here on the tourist run for pictures. It's a habit with them, but I don't understand why Jesse didn't keep them moving along like he was supposed to. You two wait inside," he said, opening the stagecoach door and exiting. "I'll go check it out."

Denise moved closer to Felicity's window, and the two of them watched as Jesse dismounted from the driver's seat. They listened in as Jim examined the horses and harness.

"I couldn't go anywhere," Jesse said in disgust. "The reins to the lead horses just fell away. They've been tampered with—cut—and I didn't catch it earlier. Seth's going to have my hide for sure."

"It wasn't your fault," Jim replied, holding up the leather. "This was a clever piece of work. Whoever ruined the reins knew the horses would stop here from habit. This take is ruined."

"Does that mean I don't get to be on TV?" Denise asked worriedly. "I told everyone at school I would."

Felicity gently patted the girl's shoulder. "I suppose they'll fix the reins and we'll continue out to the mines. We'll just be delayed, that's all."

She pushed open the door and started to climb out of the stage to consult with the Colts, but at that moment one of the chartered cars carrying tourists drove over a particularly sharp piece of rock. The explosion of the worn tire boomed off the mountain walls, startling the cast, the crew, and worst of all, the horses.

With neighs of terror, the horses gathered themselves for an instinctive flight from danger. Sixteen muscled legs bunched and exploded into pure animal speed, and Felicity was thrown back against the seat, while Denise was tossed to the floor.

"Mommy!" Denise screamed as she slid toward the still-open door. Felicity grabbed her.

"I've got you, Denise!" she yelled above the noise of the wooden wheels and the pounding hoofs. "Hold on to me tight. We'll slow down in no time."

"There's no driver. We left him behind," Denise sobbed as her fingers tightened on Felicity's skirt.

Felicity was holding Denise with one arm, and the window frame with the other. The stage was bouncing wildly, and her silk hat slipped from her hair and went bouncing out the open door. Felicity watched it go, and wished with all her heart that she was on solid ground with it. She debated the possibility of jumping with the child in her arms, but their speed was already too fast and increasing all the time. She felt panic rise in her throat.

"Felicity! Are you two all right?"

Her head jerked up at the familiar voice. Seth was outside her window, keeping pace with the speeding stage in his Jeep. The top was down, and beside him sat Jim.

"Yes!" she screamed back with relief, still holding tightly to Denise and the window frame.

"Jim's going to try and mount one of the lead horses and stop you. It may get a bit rough, so hold on tight, okay?"

"Right!" Felicity answered more confidently than she felt. She looked ahead and her heart sank. The dirt road ran through the open meadows and ended at an abandoned mine. The horses would injure themselves at this breakneck speed. Even if they managed to turn away from the old mining structures at the last minute, the passengers of the driverless coach still stood the risk of injury.

"I'm ready," Jim yelled to Seth, and Seth nodded his acknowledgment. His forehead was furrowed as he concentrated on driving the rocky dirt course. Carefully Seth aligned the Jeep with the two lead horses.

Felicity pushed Denise behind her, safely wedging the child between her body and the opposite side of the stage. She then craned her neck to watch Jim stand on the seat of the Jeep, grab Seth's shoulder for support, and tense for the leap.

The shadow of the mountains was now closer than ever, signaling the end of the meadow. The horses showed no signs of tiring, and their muscles pushed under sweat-slicked coats for even more speed to escape the pursuing vehicle.

Seth kept the Jeep perfectly aligned for Jim. Fortunately the horses' momentum was far too great to allow them to turn away from the vehicle. Jim let go of Seth's shoulder, then leapt for the back of the near lead horse.

Felicity screamed in horror, fearing he wouldn't make it, but Jim's jump was timed perfectly. He landed solidly astride the horse. Seth pulled up at Felicity's scream, his face white as he slowed the Jeep to get the passengers in his line of sight. His quick check showed that Felicity and Denise were unharmed, and some of his color returned.

"He made it, Felicity," Seth yelled, "but I don't know if he can stop the horses in time."

"Will he get hurt?" Felicity shivered, her hair flying about her face.

"He has a better chance than you two. You'll both have to come with me. Jim should be able to slow the horses enough for you to chance it."

Felicity wasn't sure she'd heard him right. Gravel from the tires and the wagon wheels spit and pinged against the metal frame of the Jeep.

"You mean *jump*?" Her eyes opened wide, but one look at the approaching mountain showed that Seth was right. Jim had slowed the horses, but they weren't about to stop.

"Hurry, Felicity!" Seth urged.

Felicity took a deep breath. "Come on, Denise," she said. "We have to get off."

The child was frozen with fear, and Felicity had to drag her into position. Their long dresses flapped in the rush of air as Felicity positioned the child in front of her, one arm around her waist, and the other steadying herself against the rocking of the coach.

"Do you think you can jump to the Jeep, Denise? Seth will catch you."

Seth was in position, the Jeep perfectly aligned, but Denise shook her head and clung to Felicity with all her strength.

"Come on, sweetheart. I'll bet the cameras are rolling right now," Felicity cajoled wildly. "Wouldn't this look great on TV? Think what all your friends in school would say. Besides, your mom's waiting for you. Don't you want to see your mother?"

Denise nodded at that, and slowly loosened her death grip on Felicity's dress.

"I'm going to throw you to Seth, okay? He'll catch you, I promise." Felicity braced her feet against the opposite seat frames. "Ready? Jump!"

Denise screamed as Felicity lifted and hurled her tiny body through the air at the Jeep. The child flailed wildly, but Felicity's throw was accurate enough for Seth to catch her and steady her for a harmless landing on the vehicle's seat.

"Get on the floor, Denise! We need room for Felicity to jump," Seth ordered, for the Jeep only had front seats, and he didn't dare take the time to stop and let the child off. There was precious little of the dirt path left.

The child did as she was told, and Felicity stood alone in the wildly rocking doorway.

"Damn!" Seth swore violently as more rocks in the meadow caused him to swerve away from the stagecoach. Felicity's breath caught in her throat, and it seemed an eternity before the vehicle was realigned with the door.

"Jump, Felicity, now!" Seth yelled when he was once again in position.

Felicity studied the distance between them, then stared at the rushing ground beneath her feet. The distance looked much wider than it did when she'd thrown Denise into the Jeep.

"Don't look at the ground, look at the Jeep! Look at me! Now, Felicity! We're running out of room!" But Felicity couldn't bring herself to leave the stage. Her hands seemed frozen in place on the door frame, and her legs refused to work. Her frantic eyes locked with his, her refusal plain to see.

"Jump, you fool, or I'll make sure the whole world knows what a coward you are!" He half-rose and, holding the steering wheel with his left hand, he extended his right toward her.

Felicity's heart lurched. She was in danger of dying, thanks to his friends, and he had the nerve to insult her! She took a deep breath, ignored her fears, and launched herself into space.

Her blue brocade swirled in the rushing air, while buttons from her boots snapped free at the force from her jump. For one horrible instant she thought she'd miscalculated, and she closed her eyes to block out the waiting granite floor. But then she felt Seth's hand clamp her arm, felt him pull her over the side of the Jeep to safety.

Just as he slammed her down onto the leather passenger seat, the left front wheel of the stagecoach struck an outcropping. The coach flipped off its two left wheels, balanced on the two right ones for a teetering second, then crashed onto its side, the wood shattering on impact.

Seth jammed on his brakes, allowing the stagecoach to get ahead. A short distance later, the horses, burdened by the massive dead weight, finally slowed to a sweating, trembling stop.

The next few minutes were a blur to Felicity. She closed her eyes and concentrated on catching her breath. She vaguely remembered helping Denise crawl up onto her lap, the sirens of the unneeded ambulances, the sounds of people being pushed back, the frantic blowing of the winded horses, which had miraculously, remained on their feet and were unharmed. Jim Colt, too, was safe. And then Denise's mother appeared at the Jeep, thanking her and Seth over and over as she took the child in her arms.

Seth opened his door and raced around to open Felicity's. He pulled her into his rough embrace. "You're all right. Thank God you're all right," he said fiercely. He held her tight against him, whispering, "I was so afraid for you." His normally tanned face had faded to a sickly color, and Felicity could feel the racing of his heart against her chest.

A slow, burning anger started to cut through the numbness of her body. She lifted her head from his shoulder and looked up into his face.

"Seth, that child could have been killed. The reins were tampered with."

Seth's face turned a shade whiter. "No."

"Yes, Jim said so. He saw."

Seth's hands tightened on her. "Felicity, I'm sure the unexpected stop was only meant to delay the commercial. I'd bet my life that this part wasn't planned. I never suspected this would happen. If I had, I'd never have let you set foot inside that stage."

"We could have been killed!" Felicity swallowed, trying to control her trembling voice. "You said you could control your friends! First they stole the costumes, and now look what happened!"

A pulse throbbed visibly in Seth's temple. "This was a true accident, Felicity. Someone had a tire blow, and the noise spooked the horses. Otherwise they would have stood quietly at their accustomed stop until the reins were repaired. I was watching all the time. I came after you, and no one was hurt. It's all over."

"Is it really?" Felicity angrily shook free of his grasp. "What happens the next time?"

"There won't be a next time." Seth's face was harsh with determination. "I promise to put a stop to all this."

"Save your promises, because I'm making one of my own." Felicity's face was as resolute as Seth's. "I'm going to put a stop to all this *myself*."

CHAPTER FIVE

"YOU CAN'T!" Seth insisted, gripping her arm before she could step away. "You won't!"

"You just watch me," Felicity hissed back. "I'm willing to turn my head and look the other way when it comes to a few dogs and some harmless tennis balls, but not when an innocent child is nearly killed! Not to mention my own close call! I can't remain silent about your friends any longer!"

"Felicity, you have to! You don't know what's at stake! Let me explain—" But Seth didn't get that chance. The rest of the crowd had finally caught up to them.

"Is everything all right over here, Seth?" It was Bill, accompanied by two paramedics. "Felicity, how are you?" he asked frantically.

"She's fine," Seth answered for her. "I was just about to drive her back to town."

"I'd rather go with Bill," Felicity asserted, trying to yank her arm free of Seth's grip. He refused to let go.

"You really should be checked over by the paramedics," Bill agreed. "Besides, our insurance policy requires it."

"I wouldn't want to interfere with established policy," Felicity said, glaring at Seth. She felt anxious to escape from him—before he could change her mind.

"It's settled, then. Come with me," Bill ordered.

Reluctantly Seth let her go, and Felicity ignored the urgency in his eyes. The sooner she could get away from him and over to the local sheriff's office, the better. She quickly climbed inside the ambulance, which already held Denise, in her mother's arms, and Jim. They wore the same shaken expression as she did, but they, too, had escaped uninjured—thanks to Seth.

If not for Seth, they might all be lying on stretchers instead of comfortably seated. Felicity hardened her heart. Seth had promised to stop his friends. It was because of Seth's insistence on her silence that all of this had happened in the first place.

Felicity kept miserably silent, glad when she was back in town, examined by the doctor, then released to go to the wardrobe building to change. Her legs felt weak and shaky as she climbed the stairs to discard the blue brocade in favor of her jeans and pullover sweater. Mechanically she creamed the heavy makeup from her face, brushed out the elaborate hairdo, and then checked her jeans pocket for her hotel key. She'd given up carrying a purse whenever she had to spend the day in costume.

When Felicity was ready to leave, she peered anxiously down the steps that led to the street. Seth was nowhere in sight, and with any luck, she might be able to inquire where the sheriff's office was and file a report. And then she was going to call Sherri and Miles in the hope that their baby had arrived. That would be reason enough for her to leave without confronting Seth again. She didn't think she could bear that.

The sun was setting as Felicity stepped outside and descended the stairs. The appearance of four old men took her momentarily by surprise. Then irritation set in. Seth had apparently sent her a welcoming party instead of coming here in person.

"Evening, Miss." It was Emil.

"Evening, Miss," Walt, Vern and Mike chorused.

Emil cleared his throat. "Seth was wondering if you'd mind stopping by Flo's for a minute." The four men surrounded her, two of them offering her an arm each.

"Do I have any choice?" Felicity asked stiffly.

"Afraid not, Miss," said Emil. "Sorry."

Felicity exhaled heavily. Two kidnappings in one week! They would never believe it back home. She could scarcely believe it herself. And to think her parents and doctor had sent her here to rest and recuperate!

"Lead on," Felicity said resignedly, although she refused to take either of the arms offered her.

Flo's drugstore had closed uncharacteristically early, Felicity noticed. Only Flo and Seth were inside. The men left Felicity at the door and politely bade her good-night.

Flo let Felicity in, then let herself out and locked the door. Felicity and Seth were alone.

"Come and sit down, Felicity." Seth had a folding chair ready for her. "I know you've had a rotten day. You look ready to drop."

Felicity *felt* ready to drop. Even worse, she couldn't ignore the crashing beginnings of another headache. "I'll sit down, but I don't intend to stay long," she said stiffly. "I don't appreciate being shanghaied, either. I know you put those men up to it."

"I needed to talk to you, and we didn't have a chance earlier." Seth studied her, his expression revealing his concern. "I had the doctor call me right after he checked you out. He said you were okay. Are you?"

"I'm in one piece. And considering the afternoon's events, that's a lot to be thankful for."

"I'm sorry about today, Felicity," he said with feeling. "I was just as surprised as you when the reins broke, especially since I had the Colt brothers check out all the tack. I would never have let you get on that stage if I'd had any idea of the danger."

"I believe you." Felicity sighed wearily. "But that doesn't change the fact that harmless pranks can backfire, just like they did today. Sooner or later someone's going to get hurt. Something has to be done about this."

"Something *has* been done. While you were with the doctor, I found and talked to all the men involved. They only wanted the reins to break so the horses would stop the stage out of habit for the usual photograph break and delay the filming. They were scared to death when that blown tire spooked the horses. Mike and Vern have given me their word that they won't be involved in any more pranks. Walt won't drop any more tennis balls, and Emil's already making arrangements to have the missing costumes replaced."

"If he hadn't stolen those costumes, I wouldn't have been in a runaway stagecoach in the first place," Felicity retorted.

"Don't think I haven't realized that. Rest assured that Emil and the others have heard exactly how I feel about their part in this latest fiasco." His eyes flashed dangerously.

Felicity almost felt sorry for the luckless old men, but she refused to be appeased. "That isn't the issue here. Those men have to be stopped. I'm sorry, but you might as well know that I intend to report all four of them to the sheriff, and that will be the end of it."

She rose from her chair and walked toward the door. But when she tried the handle, nothing happened. She whirled to face Seth.

"One thing about these old locks," Seth observed calmly, "you need keys to get in *and* out." He held the key in front of her, then said, "I can't let you report them, Felicity. There's much more at stake here than ruined commercials."

"What? What could be so important that you'd risk the safety of people you obviously care about? Like Denise and Jim and Jesse?" *And what about me?* she thought. "We could all have been killed today."

"I know. I was there, too, remember? But for your own protection, it's better that you don't know."

"Oh, I see," Felicity snapped. "I'm supposed to believe that you know best, and look the other way again."

"I'm asking you to trust me, Felicity."

"The last time I did that I ended up on a runaway stagecoach with a screaming child in my arms. I'm not anxious to repeat the experience."

"You won't, if you keep quiet," Seth said firmly.

"And if I don't, what do you plan to do? Keep me locked up in Flo's for the rest of my vacation?"

"The question isn't what *I'd* do." Seth's face was impassive. "It's what the others would do."

Felicity felt herself go cold at the look on his face. "Which is?" Her voice was barely a whisper.

"You may be able to report Emil and his friends. You may even send them to jail. But if they go, they'll take you with them."

"You're just trying to scare me," Felicity scoffed. "You yourself told me those men didn't want the commercials made because of the summer tourists. They want Silverton like it was in the old days—a quiet, sleepy little town year round. I'm not an old-timer. I'm not even a resident. No one would believe I was involved."

Seth's gaze was deadly serious. "Who ruined the *first* commercial take, Felicity?" he asked with emphasis.

Felicity gasped as the meaning of his question sank in.

"It wasn't any of *my* friends," Seth said. "They didn't fall on their rear ends in a saloon-girl outfit while the camera was trained on them."

Felicity's hand rose to her throat in disbelief. "That was an accident! You know it was an accident! If I hadn't fallen, Vern and Mike would have released those dogs and ruined the take just the same!"

"You know that and I know that, but does anyone else? You've been seen with me and with the local residents. What if the sheriff believes that you were in on the plots to ruin the commercials, too?"

"You'd . . . you'd actually tell them that?" Her heart twisted at his threat.

"No, I wouldn't. And I'd do everything in my power to see that no one else would, either." For a split second, Seth's face took on a blazing intensity. "But there's a lot at stake here, and Emil and the others might resent your interference enough to make trouble for you."

"They'd send me to jail, even though I'm innocent?" Felicity asked in shock. She seemed to be little more than a pawn in an unfamiliar game.

"They might, if you pushed them far enough. I was able to get their solemn promise to stop sabotaging the commercials, but their backs are against the wall. I don't know how much more I could do if you go to the sheriff. Please, Felicity, for your own sake, keep quiet."

Felicity couldn't believe what she was hearing. "Those sweet old men would send me to jail?"

"Felicity—" Seth approached her, one hand reaching for hers "—you won't go to jail, not if I have anything to say about it. But I do need your cooperation."

Felicity shrank from his touch, ignoring the tight, closed look on his face. "I want to leave," she said dully. "My head hurts."

Seth immediately unlocked the door. "I'll drive you back to your hotel. You don't look well," he said with sudden worry.

She shook her head, the movement sending spasms of pain through her temples. "I'd rather you didn't," she insisted. She turned and left Flo's, unaware that Seth was following her, unaware that he kept a close watch until she stepped inside the hotel.

Her room was a haven of calm and quiet. Felicity collapsed onto the bed, the pounding headache insignificant compared to the heartache she felt. Her disillusionment with Seth was as sharp, as cutting as a knife. Unconsciously, she'd been treasuring every moment she spent with him, but what kind of man would have friends who threatened to put her in jail—friends who committed acts of vandalism, sabotage and theft? True, he didn't seem to be involved, but still...

Felicity rubbed her temples, trying to dispel some of the pain. Why did life have to be so difficult? No wonder her brother had run off to live like a hermit in the mountains. Except that if she ran away from Silverton, she'd want to take Seth with her....

Miles. Felicity checked her watch, pulled herself into a sitting position and picked up the phone for her nightly call. She had yet to get through to him. Perhaps Sherri had already had her baby. That would be welcome news right now. Just the sound of a loving family voice would be a comfort. Anything to soothe her raw nerves and to distract her from the pain in her head.

"Rocky Mountain ranger station. Barrett speaking," came the deep, familiar tones.

"Miles!" Felicity could hardly believe her luck. She quickly wiped the tears from her cheeks and tried to steady her voice.

"It's me—Felicity. I've been trying to reach you all week!"

"The phones have been out. It's good to hear from you!"

"It's good to hear from you, too," Felicity said warmly. "How's Sherri? And the baby? Or has she had it yet? Can you talk, or are you busy?"

Felicity heard her brother laugh. "No, I'm not busy, yes, I can talk, and my wife and baby-to-be are fine. In fact, the doctor says they're both disgustingly healthy. Although the baby is being particularly stubborn about making his or her grand appearance."

Felicity sighed. "I was hoping the baby had been born and I could come see you."

There was a pause on the line. "You don't sound too cheerful. Not enjoying your vacation? Mother told me about your headaches. How are they?"

"Still here," Felicity reluctantly admitted, wincing at the one that was bothering her now. "But I didn't call to complain. I just wanted to leave you my number so you can reach me when the baby comes."

"And to hear a familiar voice?" Miles guessed.

"Yes, that, too. It's awfully lonely in these mountains, Miles. How do you stand it?"

Felicity wished she could withdraw the question. Her brother was a very private person, and she'd probably presumed on their relationship too much. But after a moment Miles answered.

"I have Sherri, Felicity. How could I be lonely?"

"Oh." Somehow that made Felicity feel even worse about her own situation. When she left here, who would she have to chase away the loneliness?

"You sound like you have a good old-fashioned case of homesickness," Miles said briskly. "Well, I have something that may cheer you up. Sherri's next doctor's appointment is in Durango, two days from now."

"Durango? That's not far from here," Felicity realized with excitement.

"Not far at all. Why don't you take the train down and we can meet you at the station? Let me just check the schedules. Yes...we'd have plenty of time to pick you up after Sherri's appointment if you take the second trip out of Silverton. Unless the baby's born between now and then, we can all go out for lunch. Sherri eats like a lumberjack lately. I can promise you a big meal, if nothing else."

"That sounds great," Felicity said.

She was almost certain Bill would give her the day off. She hadn't told anyone from home about her job, and she didn't want to tell Miles, afraid that it might get back to her parents. But she did want to see her brother. That acting job was playing havoc with her life in more ways than one. If it wasn't for the fact that she'd met Seth as a result, she would have heartily wished she'd never taken the position in the first place.

"Give me the trip number and departure time, Miles. I don't have a train schedule handy. If I can be there, I will," she promised.

Miles read it to her, and Felicity quickly memorized the information. Working for Barrett Shipping had, if nothing else, given her a head for numbers.

"Okay. Sherri and I will be looking forward to seeing you, unless..."

"Unless Mother Nature has other plans." Felicity smiled. Her quiet, reserved brother actually sounded excited.

"I have to go, Felicity. I can't tie up the line for too much longer."

"I understand. Tell Sherri I said hello, and give her my love."

"I will. Goodbye." Miles rang off with his characteristic brevity, and Felicity reluctantly replaced the receiver.

How happy Miles had sounded, she thought. How his voice sang out when he talked of his wife and his baby-to-be. And how awful that she should be so terribly, terribly jealous.

Still, talking with Miles had made her head feel better. Maybe that know-nothing doctor of hers was right. Maybe her headaches were all emotionally triggered. *Great,* she thought to herself. *Not only am I in a crazy town involved with a crazy man, but I may be crazy myself!*

As if to confirm her suspicions, her headache left immediately. Felicity frowned, then couldn't refrain from smiling. If only all her problems could be so accommodating. Picking up the phone again, she ordered herself some dinner, then showered off the dust from her afternoon's adventure while she waited for room service.

As she reached into the chest of drawers for some night clothes, she noticed that the paperbacks she had resolved to pack and give away to her nephews were still sitting out. She ran her fingers over them, then gently placed them on her nightstand. Somehow the man who wrote about honesty and decency in the Old West didn't quite match up with the man of today—the man who was protecting his small-town friends by hiding their illegal activities. She decided to read all of Decker Townsend's Western novels. Somewhere, she had to find the missing pieces of the puzzle that was Seth Tyler.

If Seth was as bad as his troublemaker friends, then heaven help him, she vowed. And if he rang as true-blue as the sterling heroes in his books... Felicity bit her lower lip, remembering the feel of his own lips against hers. Then heaven had better help her instead.

FELICITY REPORTED to work early the next morning, only to discover that the day's shooting schedule had been changed. The insurance company had refused to allow any retakes of the stagecoach commercial, so Bill was forced to shoot a different scene at the old mines, one that required only the male actors. That left Felicity with a much-needed day off.

She returned to the hotel, went back to bed for a long nap, then rose and had a leisurely breakfast. Next, she decided to do some shopping. Felicity had promised her two nephews souvenirs; she also needed a selection of appropriate gifts for Sherri and the new baby.

Her morning was spent roaming the shops and searching for presents. Felicity found that task easy, for it seemed everyone in town knew she had helped rescue Denise from the runaway stagecoach. Felicity grew embarrassed listening to everyone's praise, but she welcomed the advice that led her to the stores with the largest assortment of children's things. Everyone was eager to hear about her two nephews, about the baby on the way, and to suggest gift ideas for them.

The warm recognition and the kind treatment she received helped soothe the nerves Seth Tyler had definitely set on edge, and by midafternoon she returned to her hotel room laden with tasteful gifts. A sandwich and a glass of milk provided by room service quickly refreshed her. Felicity then changed from her sneakers into sturdy walking boots and grabbed a jacket, stuffing into its pocket Seth's new paperback, which she'd started the night before.

One of the merchants she met during her shopping trip had recommended a walking tour of the area and had given Felicity a map.

"You're certain I won't get lost?" she'd asked.

"Oh, no. You'll stay in sight of the town the whole way. But it's a little different from the usual tourist stuff."

Felicity could tell she was being distinguished from the regular visitors, and knew that was a compliment.

"Thank you. It'll be a nice change. Back home all I hiked were office corridors."

The walk started at the train station and continued on toward the outskirts of town. Felicity found the footpath easy enough to follow, and gloried in the silence of the outdoors. A few hundred feet away from the town, near the shores of the river and the edge of the mountains, one could almost believe that civilization had been left behind forever. But if she simply turned around, she could see the town, which reassured her that she was in no danger of getting lost.

A few hours later Felicity found a particularly welcoming nook, a clearing nestled in the pine forest. She spread the jacket she'd brought on the ground, then sat down. She reached into her pocket and withdrew Seth's paperback and an apple saved from lunch, and began to read.

Surely books revealed something of their authors, Felicity thought. She was determined to read this one with an eye toward analyzing Seth's character. But as the afternoon passed, Felicity found herself being drawn into the magic of the story. She caught herself again and again imagining Seth as the hero and herself as the heroine.

After several unsuccessful attempts to stop projecting the two of them into the book's love scenes, Felicity gave up reading. It was time to put aside imagination and face reality. And reality told her she was falling in love with Seth Tyler. He was occupying more and more of her heart every day. And that made her desperate to know if he was Seth Tyler, accessory to sabotage, or Seth Tyler, town savior.

Sighing heavily, Felicity flipped to the last page. As she suspected, the hero and heroine were rewarded with a happy ending. If only her life could be so simple. She closed the book and slipped it back into the jacket pocket. She'd finish it later, she decided, as she carefully buried the apple core in the soil.

She stood up, brushing the pine needles off her jacket, when a sudden shadow crossed her face. She instinctively looked up and saw Seth.

"Hello, Felicity. Some friends of mine told me I'd find you here." He moved toward her, reaching out a hand to help with the jacket.

"Hello, Seth. Isn't anything secret in this town?" Felicity fought to disguise her delight at seeing him, but her voice still sounded more eager than she'd intended. To compensate, she ignored his hand, and pulled on the jacket herself.

Seth abruptly dropped his arm. "Not much," he admitted. "But there are still a few things you don't know. I'd like to fill you in, if you're willing to listen."

Felicity tried to work the zipper with trembling hands. "It all depends. Did your friends give you their permission?" she asked, unable to keep the slight acid tone from her voice.

"I don't need anyone's permission but yours. Are you willing to listen to me or not?"

CHAPTER SIX

"I'M WILLING," Felicity immediately agreed.

Seth nodded, apparently satisifed with her response, and led her a short distance away to a natural rock formation that provided hard but comfortable seats. He gestured for her to sit, then sat down beside her.

"What do you know about uranium?" he asked suddenly.

"Uranium?" Felicity echoed. She shrugged. "I have the usual general knowledge, I suppose. Why?"

"Then bear with me for a moment. It's important. Uranium never occurs naturally in the free state. It's found as an oxide or a complex salt such as pitchblende or carnotite. Most of our country's uranium ore is mined in the Rocky Mountains."

Felicity nodded her understanding, curious about where this lecture on mineralogy was leading.

"The highest-grade uranium ore in the United States is found in a mineral called coffinite. Coffinite is made up of over sixty percent uranium, and was discovered right here."

"In Colorado?" Felicity asked in surprise.

"That's right." Seth's tone was decidedly gloomy. "The gold rush and the silver rush were replaced by the uranium rush. There's a ready, high-paying market for it with the government. What's more, uranium can be easily detected with a Geiger counter, even in the hands of the most inexperienced prospector.''

''What does this have to do with Silverton, Seth?'' Felicity asked.

Seth glanced toward the town, then back at Felicity. ''Jesse's wife, Sara, works for a dentist. One of her jobs is to scan the X-ray room periodically to check the radiation level. Imagine her surprise a few months ago when her Geiger counter went berserk.''

Felicity waited eagerly for Seth to go on.

''At first she thought her counter was defective, as the X-ray machines had just been serviced. It turned out that her young son had visited her at lunch, and had left an unusually shaped rock on her desk. He'd picked it up while hiking, and wanted her to use it as a paperweight. It was uranium.''

''What an incredible surprise!'' Felicity's eyes sparkled.

''Oh, yes, it was a surprise, all right,'' Seth replied grimly. ''A most unwelcome one.''

''But why, Seth? This is a mining town. You told me some of the residents still work the old silver and gold mines to make their living. But uranium! They could all be rich! Why wouldn't the town be happy over such a find?''

Seth's eyes glittered angrily. ''Think, Felicity, *think!* Who has sole rights to all uranium in this country?''

''The government does, of course.''

''That's right. And who is the biggest government user of uranium?''

''That would be the military, I suppose,'' Felicity answered.

''Right again. Now, what do you think is going to happen to this little town when the government finds out there's uranium in our mountains? Do you think they're going to sit back and let us do their mining for them?''

"Wouldn't they?" Felicity asked uneasily.

Seth sprang from his perch, as though unable to sit still any longer. "The hell they would. You know, most people don't own the mineral rights on their land. Anyway, haven't you ever heard of the law of Eminent Domain? That entitles the government to take any land away from its owner in the best interests of the nation. They'd be in here so quick it wouldn't even be funny. And the rest of us would be out!"

"Surely you exaggerate!" Felicity protested. "Besides, you'd all be reimbursed, probably with more money than you realize. Think of the exciting new future you could have!"

Seth grabbed her shoulders, and gazed into her eyes. "Felicity, we don't want a new future!" he said urgently. "We don't want to be turned out of our homes! All the gold and silver miners in this town could lose their mines and their livelihood. Sure, some of them might be employed by the government, but they'd never regain their independence. They'd never be their own masters again."

"But you can't just throw away the opportunity for growth and expansion! Wouldn't some of the town remain?"

Seth released her, and turned to follow her gaze. "What town? There certainly wouldn't be a tourist trade once the government installed the strict security measures all uranium mines require. And our train would once again be used for ore shipments, not passengers."

"I can see what you're saying, Seth, but to throw away a fortune! Can't you find *any* good reason for reporting the uranium find?" she pleaded.

"No," was the stark answer. "The disadvantages far outweigh the advantages. Besides," he said, "it may not be a fortune. We've only discovered the ore on Emil's land."

"Emil's?"

Seth nodded. "That's right. I took Sara Colt's Geiger counter and backtracked the area her son had hiked. I can't speak for what's below the ground, but the visible deposit of ore is Emil's land outside town. He'd be the only one making any money. The rest of us would just be reimbursed for our property. The gold and silver miners might make a little money out of the deal, but the merchants would be ruined. Their main resource is Silverton's summer visitors. Once those are banned, there won't be much left of their businesses."

Felicity asked the obvious question. "Seth, how does this tie in with the sabotage of the commercials? You wouldn't have told me all this unless there was some connection."

"There's a connection, all right." Seth rejoined her on the rock, settling his body beside hers. "Originally, only Jesse and his wife knew about the uranium. They decided to take his brother, Jim, into their confidence. Jim knew I'd done some mineralogy courses in college, and he trusted me to keep quiet. So I went to Emil's with the Geiger counter."

Seth grimaced at the memory. "I thought I was being quiet, but Emil's an old woodsman and he spotted me in a minute. And of course he demanded to know what I was up to. With a screaming Geiger counter in my hand, it wasn't too hard to figure out."

Felicity touched his arm lightly. "And then?"

"Well, at first it wasn't so bad," Seth said. "Emil believed in keeping the whole thing quiet, as I did. He didn't want to sell his land. He and Flo have been friends for a long time, so he did tell her about the uranium. A few weeks went by, and all seemed fine. Then the people from the department of tourism decided to film their commercials here. Emil fell to pieces.''

''Was he worried that more tourists would increase the chances of the uranium being discovered?''

''Exactly,'' Seth confirmed. ''Even though Emil doesn't live right in town, he still gets lots of tourists on his land in the summer. There's some old mines just adjoining his property, and naturally a lot of visitors like playing prospector. The mines are perfectly safe—they're kept up as a tourist attraction—but of course there isn't any gold or silver left in them. Every summer some of those people end up on Emil's property in their search for gold or silver. It seems like we always get a few tourists with gold fever. And Geiger counters . . .''

''No wonder Emil was upset. Is that why he decided to put a stop to the commercials?''

''Yes. I found out that he'd convinced three of his friends to help him.''

''Did he tell them about the uranium, too?'' It seemed to Felicity that too many people were finding out about Emil's uranium strike.

''No, thank goodness. Walt, Mike and Vern all hate the tourist season. They're retired miners who remember the so-called good old days. Emil merely played on those feelings, feelings they knew Emil himself shared. They agreed to help him ruin the commercials so that the film people would leave town.''

''But Seth, all Emil's going to do is draw *more* attention to Silverton, and to himself, if he's caught! That's the last thing he should want.''

"For some reason, Emil refuses to acknowledge that risk. What's worse, the tourism people have a lot of resources available, and if they ever decided those ruined commercials are more than harmless pranks and bad luck, they could request a full investigation. Frankly, I don't think Emil could stand the pressure. He's at the end of his rope as it is—especially after I finished with him today." Seth's fist clenched. "When I saw that stagecoach take off with you and Denise inside it . . ."

He drew in a deep, shuddering breath, and Felicity knew he was remembering the sound of wood crashing and splintering on the jutting rocks.

"After Emil tampered with the reins, friend or no friend, I could have killed him with my bare hands." The fury on Seth's face was frightening to see. "If nothing else, at least that near-disaster scared the living daylights out of all of them. And if that didn't, I did. I know for a fact they won't try anything else."

Seth paused, then asked in a calm, reasonable voice, "Now can you see why I didn't want you to go to the police with this?"

"In a way," Felicity answered slowly. "Although I still can't really see why you want to pass up such a golden opportunity for progress and advancement."

Seth's eyes clouded, and Felicity had the feeling he was disappointed in her.

"I promise to keep the uranium discovery a secret," she quickly offered. It was against her better judgment, but she had to erase that terrible look in his eyes. "I simply find it hard to believe that a handful of people are secretly making a decision that affects eight hundred other people," she said logically, eager to defend herself. "It seems to me that the rest of the town should be consulted."

"Don't be so naive, Felicity! First of all, Emil could be making a big fuss over nothing. I have a call in to a mineralogist friend of mine. He's on another project right now, but when he finishes that, he'll come here to do a discreet survey of Emil's uranium deposit for me. That deposit could be the proverbial flash in the pan, which would make all this speculation purely academic."

"And if it's a bona-fide vein? What then?"

"We'll cross that bridge when we come to it," Seth said determinedly. "In the meantime, I have no intention of informing the town until the survey is done. I know that eight hundred people couldn't keep this secret. One greedy person could ruin it for all of us."

"I don't think that wanting progress is the same thing as being greedy," Felicity insisted. "You're the one being naive. This town isn't going to disappear off the map with the uranium mining. The government workers will need the services Silverton can provide, including mining manpower. The way you describe it, the town's going to be razed to the ground!" Couldn't Seth see the mistake he was making?

"No, but our quiet way of life would, and to most of us, that's the same thing."

Felicity crossed her arms. "What way of life? A basic existence in the middle of nowhere, where everyone struggles to get through the winter? With uranium mining, the town wouldn't have to depend on worn-out silver mines and the tourist trade for its income. How can Silverton afford to pass up that kind of security? After all, not everyone can make a living writing books, you know."

"My personal income has nothing to do with it! I should have known you wouldn't understand. I don't know why I bothered to tell you all this in the first place."

The bitter words were flung out in a way that reduced Felicity to the status she'd had when they first met. Again she was an outsider, and she didn't like that feeling one bit.

"I'm only saying you shouldn't presume to speak for the rest of the town, that's all. I'm going back to the hotel now." Felicity held her temper in check as she rose and brushed the dust off her jeans.

"Sure, run away, Felicity. Soon you'll be back in the big city with the bright lights. A *basic* little town like this is too frightening for the likes of you."

Felicity froze, her brushing hands suddenly still. "I'm not afraid of this place."

"Yes, you are. You bury yourself in your work and your big-city distractions to avoid facing the fact you're lonely. That's why you're so concerned about modernizing our little town. You can't understand how we can live full, satisfying lives without outside distractions. There's too much time here for you to dwell on yourself and how empty your life is!"

Felicity's eyes flew wide open. She couldn't have been more stunned if he had physically hit her. When she finally regained her speech, her voice was cold with fury.

"I think you're confusing fact and fiction, Mr. Author. And if my being kidnapped twice, practically blackmailed and nearly killed are common events in this town, then perhaps a little modernization might do Silverton some good!"

Felicity spun around on the gravel and started back on the path into town. "Go ahead, then," she heard Seth call after her. "Modernize us! Tell the government about our uranium! I'm sure if you work it right, you can get a big fat finder's fee from them, too."

Felicity's heart wrenched at the insult. She stiffened her spine and hurried toward town, all the while listening in vain for Seth to call her back.

By the time she reached her hotel room, Felicity's head was pounding with an intensity that made her tremble. She grabbed the furniture for support against the dizziness and pounding in her skull, then fumbled in her purse for her painkillers. With tears in her eyes, she gulped one down, desperately praying it would start to work soon.

Gingerly, with as little motion as possible, she lowered herself onto the bed, holding her head in her hands, willing herself not to cry. No way would she let Seth's cheap gibe disturb her! Besides, getting upset about it would only make her headache worse, Felicity told herself.

And there was no denying it, her headache *was* getting worse. Felicity felt so nauseated that she lay down, but that made her head pound even more, and she was forced to sit up again.

She looked frantically around the room for a distraction. Her room had no TV or radio, in keeping with its period decor. But the pain was insistent, and finally in desperation Felicity rose from the bed and grabbed one of Seth's paperbacks. She sat back down on the bed, took off her boots and crossed her legs. Maybe a story would keep her mind off the pain.

The book, entitled *Tarnished Dreams*, was set in a small California town during the gold-rush days. The heroine was a young, single woman content with her life, while the hero was a dynamic man, unsatisfied with his lot in the sleepy little town.

Gold was discovered nearby, and suddenly everything changed. Felicity read about the heroine's shock at the town's sudden greed, her horror at watching the integrity of her friends and neighbors disintegrate before her eyes. The hero was caught up in the discovery, eagerly fighting for his claim and his share of the riches.

Slowly he changed, too, and the heroine tried unsuccessfully to show her man what was happening to him and those around them. Felicity felt the tears spring to her eyes. The town in the book could easily be Silverton, and she the blind, stubborn hero. The pain in her head increased with the strain of reading, but Felicity was captivated by the story. Had Seth known about the uranium when he'd written this?

The ominous tone hinted at some upcoming tragedy; despite that, Felicity continued reading. Sure enough, an outsider, a drunken miner, came upon the heroine while the hero was off on his claim. She was attacked, and her aging father was shot and killed while trying to protect his daughter.

More tears fell at the tragedy, but Felicity forced her wet lids open and continued to read. The hero found and killed the drunkard, but not before the man had forced himself on the heroine. The hero finally realized the price he'd paid for his desire for gold, and he left the claim, taking the heroine away with him. Their love still survived, but it would never be the same. Both of them would have to live with the memories of what had happened—and what might have been.

Tarnished Dreams fell to the floor, and Felicity finally released the sobs she had kept inside. Seth was right. The brief scare she'd suffered inside a runaway stagecoach was nothing compared to what might happen to the town if she reported the saboteurs. She would keep safe the secret he had entrusted her with.

Her temples were pounding mercilessly, and she moaned at the pain. She cradled her head in her hands, trying to force back the shuddering sobs that sent new waves of agony through her.

Seth was also right when he'd claimed that she only wanted Portland for its distractions—when he'd said she refused to face her loneliness. Yes, she *was* lonely. She had always been alone, without a soulmate, without a lover. But lots of people were, weren't they? Not everyone lived happily ever after like Sherri and Miles. At least she had her job, and she had her family, which gave her some contentment in her life. Without that, she'd be climbing the walls. No, she didn't want Silverton, but she did want Seth. Unfortunately one went with the other, and her remaining time in the mountains was quickly running out.

The pain forced her eyes closed, and Felicity rocked back and forth on the bed in agony. She wondered if she dared risk another painkiller, then wondered if anyone ever died from heartache. Headache, she corrected herself. Then another dizzying spasm hit, and she was grabbing her head to protect it before crashing to the floor.

It was there, trembling with pain on the old hooked rug, that Seth found her.

"Felicity!"

His harsh cry penetrated the foggy mists of her pain. Seth had opened the unlocked door when there was no answer to his knock. Rushing to her side, he gathered her into his arms.

"What's wrong? Answer me!" he demanded fiercely.

Felicity raised her tear-stained face to his. "My head hurts," she gasped, the room spinning as he lifted her back onto the bed and sat with her on his lap, his arms still supporting her.

"Please just leave me alone," she managed to say before another wave of pain hit. She winced, closing her eyes again as she waited for it to recede.

Seth saw her pills on the nightstand. "Did you take your medication?"

Felicity debated which would require less effort, nodding or answering. She gave a slight nod, then gasped aloud as the pain in her head redoubled.

"I'm going to call a doctor," Seth said as her already white face grew visibly paler.

Felicity opened her eyes as he tightened his arms protectively around her. "Please don't. My own doctor says these headaches have no physical cause." She tensed again as a fresh stab of pain assaulted her, and she felt Seth's hand slide into hers, offering reassurance.

When that spasm had passed, she struggled to get away from him. "Why are you here? I already told you I intend to keep quite about the pranks and the uranium. I haven't changed my mind." Her breath came in ragged gasps. She didn't want him to see her like this. But in spite of her pride, she felt her hand tighten in his as yet another onslaught of pain knifed through her.

Seth gathered her closer. "I'm not leaving, Felicity." He spoke softly, but his voice was firm. "If you don't want to call anyone, I'll stay here until this is over. You shouldn't be alone."

"I'm used to it." New tears that had nothing to do with her headache spilled onto her cheeks. "Go away. Doesn't Silverton need you? I'm sure you can't spare any time from your job as town hero."

By now Seth's face was as pale as hers. "Shh, now," he urged gently. "You're just upsetting yourself. It can't be good for your head. The sooner you get rid of the pain, the sooner I'll leave. That should be reason enough for you to cooperate." There was more sadness than sarcasm in his words, but Felicity was in no shape to notice.

All she knew was that the pain was killing her, and Seth had offered to stay. He was a life preserver tossed to her amid the waves of agony, and she'd be a fool not to take it.

She forced herself to lie quietly in his arms, letting his strong body rock her back and forth. The motion seemed to help her head instead of aggravating the pain. Little by little she started to relax. After a few moments Seth began to hum, his deep voice a comforting lullaby, and Felicity concentrated on the pleasant sound.

Slowly the pain lessened enough that her eyes didn't squeeze out tears with each new wave. Seth smiled when he saw this, gently wiping away the last of her tears with his fingertips. Felicity closed her eyes at the sweetness of that sensation and leaned her head into his hand.

"A little better?" Seth asked quietly.

Felicity was able to nod without a fresh burst of pain.

"Good." He continued his humming and rocking. A half hour passed before she finally felt the last vestiges of pain melt away. She opened her eyes and immediately found his.

"It's gone. My headache's gone," she said with wonderment. "Thank you."

"It was probably your pills," Seth replied, although his relief was evident.

"No, it was you." Felicity continued to stare into his eyes, conscious of her shoulder against his firm chest, and of her hand still tightly clasped in his.

"I'm sorry I upset you earlier," Seth said. "What I said was unforgivable. Not only was it rude, but it set off one of your headaches." He drew in a deep, unsteady breath. "Good lord, Felicity, are they always this bad?"

"They weren't back home," Felicity remembered, then instantly regretted her words. She didn't want him to feel guilty about something that was her problem, not his. "I mean," she quickly added, "it must be the high altitude and the change in location."

"It's the location, all right, but it has nothing to do with the altitude," Seth said bitterly. "I'm sorry you chose Silverton for your vacation, Felicity."

"I'm not." Her eyes were clear as she spoke the simple words. "And I don't think you are, either."

"Felicity..." He sighed heavily. "Don't look at me like that. I think I'd better leave before..." Already the worried look in his eyes was being replaced by tiny embers that threatened to flame into life.

"You take care of yourself, and try to get a good night's sleep. If you need anything, just give me a call. I'm in the phone book."

Seth bent to kiss her on the cheek, but the friendly goodbye kiss he'd obviously planned was thwarted when Felicity deliberately turned her face. His lips landed firmly, searingly, on hers. Before he could react, Felicity wound one arm around his neck and brought his hand to her heart.

Seth responded instantly, his light caress immediately changing to one of passion and desire. Felicity felt that desire, too, and responded in kind. Her lips parted, inviting deeper intimacy, but Seth backed away.

"Felicity, please..." He set her firmly away from him. "You haven't been well. I don't want to take advantage of the situation, but I'm only human. This has to stop *now*."

CHAPTER SEVEN

"Why?" Felicity asked as she sat up, feeling cold and lost without his body next to hers.

Seth reluctantly moved from the bed to the chair. "I could name a million reasons," he said, running his fingers through his hair.

"Because I'm not like Valerie, right?"

"Valerie?" Seth stared at her in astonishment. "What does she have to do with this?"

"She was a local woman and I'm not." Felicity crossed her legs and rested her hands behind her on the bed. "You're only interested in someone from Silverton."

"Felicity, wherever did you get that idea? It isn't true. I won't deny it would make things easier if you were, but there's no point in dwelling on that. No, *you're* the reason I'm in a chair instead of over there."

"Me?"

"Yes, you." Seth's glance was accusing. "You told me just the other night that you didn't want to complicate your departure. You were getting too used to my company. You were getting spoiled by me—I think that's how you put it."

Felicity flinched. Those were indeed her words.

"If I recall, you didn't want to take things any further. I think I'm correct in saying that the two of us in your bed doesn't quite fit in with those wishes."

He sounded brisk, almost curt, and Felicity flushed miserably. She hadn't wanted him to leave her side, yet Seth was right. She *had* said she didn't want to get further involved with him. But that seemed a million years ago now.

"Seth, I—"

He cut her off. "You've made your position quite clear, Felicity. You have your future, and I have mine." His voice was harsh as he stood to leave.

"But Seth, I don't want a future with only Portland and my work! I want more!" *I want you!* But she couldn't bring herself to say it out loud.

"Lady, this may come as a surprise, but you can't have it all. No one can. You've drawn up the rules for the rest of your stay and I, for one, intend to abide by them, no matter how idiotic I think they are." He glared at her.

"Now if you'll excuse me, I have to go. I'm meeting with Flo and the Colt brothers. We have business to discuss."

Felicity clenched her fists and managed to get out a neutral, "Of course." She should have known that Silverton would once again command his attention. She was no competition when it came to his crusade for his hometown.

But his next words changed her opinion. "I know Bill's still filming out at the mines tomorrow, so you won't have to work. Will you meet me for lunch? Surely that's harmless enough for you."

Felicity felt a fierce joy flood through her at his request, then dismay. "I'm going to visit my brother and his wife tomorrow. I'm taking the train to Durango," she said regretfully.

"Your sister-in-law had the baby?" he said with surprise. "But . . . that means you won't be coming back.

Well, then—" he reached inside his shirt pocket for a pen "—I want your address. And your phone numbers. Work and home," he ordered.

"That isn't necessary. She hasn't had the baby yet," Felicity explained, delighted by his request. "I'll be returning. Sherri has a doctor's appointment in Durango tomorrow, and I'm meeting them for lunch. I haven't seen my brother and his wife since they married, so I decided not to wait for the baby."

"Oh." Seth put away his pen with evident relief. "Then I'll see you when you get back." He checked his watch. "I really have to leave now, or I'll be late."

Felicity showed him to the door. "Thank you for getting rid of my headache. That was some cure," she said lightly.

"I'm glad I could help." He lingered a moment more, and just when Felicity felt certain he would kiss her, he said, "Goodbye," and was gone.

Felicity closed the door with a sense of disappointment, leaning her cheek against the wooden panel. What had just happened between them? At first she'd thought Seth was rejecting her, but then it seemed he wasn't, and now he'd rushed off again. If only she wasn't so confused. The old Felicity would simply have put Silverton and Seth Tyler behind her. An isolated old mining town with saboteurs and hidden uranium deposits was an unlikely place for a big-city businesswoman. The old Felicity would have returned to the real world of Barrett Shipping, big cities and progress. But that no longer seemed such a cheerful prospect.

She turned away from the door. Seth was right. She did want it all. Was that so wrong? She saw his book, *Tarnished Dreams*, and her bottle of prescription pills on the floor. She picked them both up, one in each hand, and stared at them for a long time.

After a few minutes Felicity placed the book on her dresser. Next she went into the bathroom and emptied her pills into the toilet. She watched as their pink, feathery trails dissolved and disappeared into the flushing swirl of water. Only then did she finally go to bed and for the first time in weeks easily dropped off to sleep.

FELICITY SHIFTED impatiently on her seat in the D&S Railroad train. She had arrived at the station right after lunch hoping to get a good seat. And hoping the train wouldn't be crowded, so she could have the whole seat to herself. She'd chosen one by the left-hand window; this was the side that allowed a view down into the Animas Canyon.

Felicity checked her watch, then stored her gifts for Sherri and the baby in the overhead racks. Fifteen more minutes until departure time. According to the schedule, the D&S left Durango in the morning, taking three hours to reach Silverton for a two-and-a-half-hour layover. Then the train left Silverton for its return trip to Durango, its last run of the day. That was the trip Felicity was making.

She would have to find other transportation back to Silverton in the evening or else stay the night in Durango and come back in the morning. She hoped to find a charter service in town, and she hadn't, therefore, brought a change of clothes. She reminded herself to call Bill later on to see how early she'd be needed on the set the next day.

Felicity adjusted her position, trying to get more comfortable. Her thoughts were once again on Seth. Last night she'd come so close to telling him how different her feelings were now. She no longer wanted to keep him at a distance, though she supposed it was still the wisest course of action. At least Seth seemed to think so, considering the speed with which he'd rushed off to his precious meeting. A whole morning later, she still hadn't recovered from her irritation at that.

Painfully, she wondered if she could choose Seth over Portland and her career. The fact that she was even acknowledging the possibility of such a choice surprised her. But somehow it felt as if she'd been heading toward this decision ever since she'd first seen him. Still, that didn't make her position any easier. She craved the intellectual stimulation of work and derived real comfort from her family's closeness. There were no jobs for her in a small town like Silverton, and life as an unemployed woman, isolated from everything familiar, was not for her. It never would be.

Felicity looked at her watch again. The train should be leaving any minute now. The conductors boarded a few last-minute stragglers and began checking tickets, and still the train didn't leave. A few of the passengers murmured among themselves, speculating on what might be causing the delay.

Felicity gazed out the window, wondering if perhaps the shipment of coal needed for the engine hadn't arrived. As her eyes swept up and down Twelfth Street, she noticed a man running to catch the train. The lone conductor remaining outside waved in recognition, waiting for the man to reach the boarding area.

Probably another local resident with connections, Felicity decided. The conductor was holding the train for him. As the man approached, Felicity started in surprise.

"Seth?" she mouthed to herself.

As if he'd heard her, Seth turned toward her window and waved. Felicity's face lit up, and she gave him a joyful smile and waved back. A moment later, the conductor opened the door to Felicity's car. As soon as Seth had hurried in, the train immediately pulled out of Silverton.

"Made it," Seth breathed out, only slightly winded from his run. "Excuse me, Miss, but is this seat taken?"

"Not at all, sir," Felicity responded, still smiling. He squeezed himself into the empty space between her and the aisle, his arm and thigh pressed pleasantly against hers.

"Tight fit, isn't it?" he asked, although that didn't seem to bother him.

"I don't mind. Seth, what are you doing here? I thought you had to work today."

"Not for long. Since Bill began filming out at the mines yesterday, he already had all my notes and recommendations for today. He only had a few more questions. I asked a friend of mine to hold the train for me, made a mad dash from the film site, and here I am."

Felicity pretended a calm she didn't feel as she asked, "Did you have important business in Durango?"

"Nothing as important as your company. Since you couldn't have lunch with me, I decided three hours with you on the train would do very nicely instead."

"Oh!" Felicity's eyes sparkled with delight.

Seth studied her face. "No hard feelings over last night?"

"Of course not. Did your meeting go well?" she asked.

"Fine, thank you," Seth replied. "I see you brought your camera."

Felicity noticed the quick change of subject, but decided not to pursue trouble just yet.

"Yes, I did. Will I seem too touristy if I take a lot of pictures?"

"No, everyone does, but they won't turn out very well because of the reflections from the glass. As soon as the train stops, we'll switch to a gondola car. They're open, and the seats face the sides instead of the front. Much better for photography."

They moved to the open gondola car during the first stop, not too far out of town. As the train started again, Felicity was ready, her camera aimed at the spectacular scenery. The train traveled along a rocky ledge hanging tenaciously from the canyon's west side, a ledge so narrow that tracks had to be specially built. The Animas River, which had been level with Silverton just outside the town, dropped lower and lower until it was four hundred feet below them. Felicity could see the year-round snow pack that fed it, and she shivered, glad she'd brought a jacket.

Seth noticed. "Cold?" he asked, for the fresh air that rushed through the open gondola held the scent of snow.

"Not really," Felicity answered as she put the camera back inside its case. "It's just that it's so...so lonely. How can anyone survive living here?"

She looked at the wild country below her. The rocky terrain seemed forbidding, yet there was life. Herds of deer and elk grazed in meadows of columbine, ready to retreat into the great pine forests at the earliest hint of danger.

"It *is* lonely, and that's part of the beauty. Fortunately the area's remained unchanged through the past century. It wouldn't be the same with crowds and concrete. But people do survive down there."

Felicity studied the rugged canyon sides and the black forests. "How?"

Seth shrugged. "It isn't easy. But you respect your environment. And you guard your tools to deal with that environment the way other people guard precious jewels. At least here, if you die it isn't by some drunk driver or someone robbing you at gunpoint for your watch and wallet. If you die in the mountains, you usually have no one to blame but yourself. It's a harsher way to live, but a more honest one."

Felicity silently thought about Sherri's baby. The child would have to learn at an early age how to take care of him or herself at the remote ranger station. When did it become too late in life to teach someone the basics? When did modern technology finally erase whatever primitive instincts for survival a person had? And then she found herself wondering if it was too late for *her* to learn.

"How did your meeting go last night?" Felicity asked again, hoping Seth wouldn't change the subject a second time.

"Not as well as I'd hoped," Seth slowly admitted. Despite the noise of the train, he lowered his voice. "My geologist friend is in town, but we still don't have the results of the uranium survey on Emil's land. It seems he's caught the flu."

"Oh, no!"

"He's in bed, sick as a dog, according to Jesse's wife. So we'll just have to sit tight until he's recovered enough to finish the survey. I don't dare call anyone else in to replace him. At least I don't have to worry about any more pranks from the old-timers." His tone became more cheerful. "I can enjoy this trip with a clear conscience."

He put his arm around Felicity's shoulders and gave her a quick squeeze. "When I'm with you Silverton takes a back seat."

"Until the results of the survey come in," Felicity said in a small, quiet voice.

Seth glanced at her sharply. "I can't abandon the town to the mercies of government uranium miners, Felicity."

"I didn't say you should," she retorted. "But what if the survey comes back, and the results report a mother lode? What then? Just how much can one man do?"

Seth had no reply for that, and Felicity felt a sudden chill that had nothing to do with the cold mountain air.

The conversation for the rest of the trip dealt strictly with the scenery. When the train drew into the Durango station, Seth escorted her back to their original car. "Are you being met, or shall I get us a cab?"

"Thank you, but I'm being met. Miles and Sherri have to be flown here from the ranger station, so they always pick up one of the ranger vehicles at the airport."

"Shall we meet later, then?"

Felicity paused in the middle of removing her packages from the overhead storage rack. "Why don't you come with me?"

"I hadn't planned on it. I assumed you wanted privacy. This is a family reunion, after all. I have a few errands to run in Durango, and then I thought I'd find a hotel. There isn't another train back to Silverton today, so I'll catch one in the morning."

"But I want you to meet my brother and sister-in-law! I know they wouldn't mind a fourth for lunch."

Seth took her packages and they joined the line in the aisle heading for the exit. "I don't think so. It would be too much of an imposition."

His refusal carried enough regret that Felicity vigorously repeated her invitation. "Please come. I'd welcome a chance to pay back some of your hospitality."

And hadn't he delayed a whole trainful of people to be with her? She felt more than just flattered.

"I'd like that," Seth replied, "but I thought you didn't want anyone to know you'd taken a job on your vacation. I can't introduce myself as the historical consultant for the commercials. Your brother's bound to wonder how we met," Seth warned. Felicity stopped in her tracks.

"Yes, he would," Felicity muttered. Her brother could always tell when she was lying, and she wasn't about to inform him of her acting job. If he found out, he'd be on the phone to her parents in record time.

"I could always introduce myself as your vacation masseur—recommended by your doctor, of course." The corners of Seth's mouth twitched with amusement at Felicity's horrified reaction.

"You can't do that! Miles still treats me like I'm ten years old! He'd die of shock and—" Seth couldn't restrain his laughter any longer, and Felicity realized he was joking. "You're awful," she said, enjoying the moment.

"I know. Come on, we're holding up the line." Seth placed his palm against her back and gently nudged her to start moving again.

"Why don't you introduce yourself as Decker Townsend?" Felicity suggested as they stepped down from the train. "I can tell them I met you while I was sight-seeing, and that you've been showing me around town. That wouldn't be a lie."

"Sounds like a good plan," Seth agreed. "But I get to tell them my real name. I have no intention of being called Decker all afternoon."

"Fair enough. Thanks, Seth," she said with relief. "I really do want you to meet them."

"There's a couple over there, waving at us." Seth pointed to a spot beyond the loading area. "Is that them?"

A second later, Felicity was flying across the distance that separated them. Joyous hugs and kisses were exchanged, then Seth arrived and introductions were made all around. They piled into the ranger vehicle for the drive to a nearby restaurant, and were soon seated at a table for four.

"I can't believe we're actually having lunch with Decker Townsend," Miles said after the first flurry of conversation had died down.

"He's read all your Westerns, Seth," Sherri declared. "And so have I."

"I like the historical accuracy," Miles said. "Your attention to detail makes the stories that much more enjoyable."

"Don't forget the romance," Sherri added with a mischievous smile. "Although I think my husband is more partial to the adventure than the kisses."

Seth gracefully accepted their compliments, offering to send them a complete set of his work.

"That's very generous of you," Sherri replied, "but we already have all your books. Give the set to Felicity," she suggested.

Miles laughed at that. "Felicity never reads fiction, and she hates Westerns. Better save yourself the trouble, Seth."

Seth gave Miles a purely masculine look of triumph. "Felicity's read two of my books so far," he remarked, "and one of them was a Western."

"Two of them were. I just finished another," Felicity corrected smugly, enjoying Seth's look of surprise, then pleasure. She didn't see Miles and Sherri take note of her animated face, and she missed the knowing look the two exchanged. She only knew that her family had a good opinion of Seth, and that meant a lot.

Sherri rose awkwardly to her feet. "I hate to leave you all in the middle of lunch, but I'm afraid I must excuse myself for a moment."

"I'll go with you, Sherri," Felicity volunteered quickly.

Once out of earshot of the men, Sherri sighed. "One of the aggravations of being pregnant is the frequent trips to the ladies room."

Felicity held open the restroom door for both of them. "I guess you'll be glad when this is all over."

Sherri patted her rounded belly as she waddled in. "It'll be nice to have my old self back, and the baby finally in my arms."

Felicity sat down in front of the mirror and touched up her makeup, and after a moment Sherri joined her.

"You look great," Felicity remarked as she studied her sister-in-law's face in the mirror. "The doctor's visit went well?"

"Oh, yes," Sherri said happily as she tidied her hair. "Mother and child are doing just fine."

Felicity nodded. She didn't see how it could have been otherwise. Sherri looked healthy and happy, even happier than Felicity remembered. There was something about Sherri that Felicity had always envied. Her serenity, she supposed. Sherri's eyes always held a look of peaceful contentment. And what was more, it seemed to be contagious, because Miles, her wild, stormy brother, had the same look.

"I'm ready, Felicity. Let's get back to the table before Miles starts worrying."

Long before they reached the table, Felicity noticed that Miles and Seth were deep in conversation. "Sherri, look at the two of them! Whatever could they be talking about?''

Sherri watched her husband, then turned toward Felicity and smiled. ''If I know Miles, he's giving Seth the third degree.''

''He wouldn't! I'll be so embarrassed if he offends him,'' Felicity wailed.

''I'm sure Miles is just playing big brother,'' Sherri said gently. ''He cares about you very much, and probably wants to get to know Seth better. We've never known you to be so interested in anyone before.''

Sherri paused delicately, not asking any personal questions, but leaving Felicity an opening to volunteer any information.

Felicity felt suddenly shy. She didn't want to talk about Seth to anyone just now. Inside, her love for him was certain enough, but the two of them sharing any kind of future seemed impossible. Unless some miraculous solution came along, it was wiser to remain silent, especially if Miles was going to play the protective big brother.

Miles caught sight of them as they approached, and the men's conversation stopped abruptly. Felicity examined Seth's face carefully, but there were no signs of anger or agitation.

''I was beginning to wonder if I should come after you,'' Miles said as he pushed in Sherri's chair. ''This close to her due date, I get nervous when she's out of my sight for long.''

''I'm doing just fine,'' Sherri assured him, and Miles gave his wife a tender smile.

''She's incredible,'' he said. ''No problems, no fussing. She just goes about her daily business, and leaves all the worrying to me.'' He reached for Sherri's hand.

"He does worry." Sherri laughed softly. "I never thought I'd see your brother nervous, Felicity."

"But aren't *you*?" Felicity asked. "You have to be flown in for your doctor's appointments. What if you went into labor back at the ranger station? It's so deserted, and the only help you'd have is the nurse at the aid station."

"All I need is Miles." Sherri smiled, turning a face so full of love to her husband that Felicity felt a sense of awe.

"And you thought Silverton was isolated, Felicity," Seth broke in. "At least we have doctors."

Miles returned his attention to Seth and Felicity. "Actually we aren't as badly off as you might think. At least we have access to aircraft. In Silverton, without a good four-wheel drive vehicle and chains, you won't be going very far in the winter. And Colorado winters last a long, long time."

"How do you like Silverton?" Sherri asked, and everyone looked at Felicity with obvious interest. Especially Seth—or so it appeared.

"It's so strange..." Felicity's eyes swept from Sherri to Miles, then back again. "Perhaps when you have someone to share it with, that makes all the difference."

Miles nodded. "All the difference in the world."

Felicity suddenly remembered how lonely and unhappy her brother had been in Portland. And yet, despite living far away from all his family and friends, he was happier now than she had ever seen him.

She gave Seth a quick look, then saw that Miles was carefully watching both her and Seth. Felicity wondered what information Miles and Seth had exchanged to make her brother watch her so closely. Miles probably did most of the talking, with Seth saying little about anything except Silverton, Felicity guessed sourly. She wondered again if she could ever be happy there. Unfortunately she was no Sherri, born and bred to the wilderness. Suddenly depressed, she toyed with her food.

"Is something wrong with your meal, Felicity?" Miles asked. "Sherri isn't eating, either."

"It's just the excitement of seeing you again." Felicity mumbled her excuse, not wanting to give the real reason. She felt unsettled, disturbed, and definitely not herself. She was afraid to admit that, despite everything, she wanted to stay in Colorado with Seth.

"Sherri?" Miles inquired.

"I think we'd better go to the hospital," Sherri said, her voice a ghost of its usual self. "I don't feel . . . quite right."

Three pairs of eyes turned toward Sherri, whose lovely face had suddenly gone quite pale, and no one noticed whose glass it was that fell to the floor and shattered.

CHAPTER EIGHT

"THEY'VE BEEN IN THERE for hours," Felicity said worriedly. Her cup of vending-machine coffee was cold and untouched as she glanced at the clock on the hospital waiting-room wall, then at her watch.

"Giving birth takes time." Seth took the cold coffee from her hand and threw it into the nearby trash can.

"I hope everything goes all right." She willed herself not to look at the clock again.

"At least your sister-in-law went into labor here in Durango near a hospital, and not out at the ranger station," Seth comforted. "That should be a load off your mind." He reached for her hand and gave it a reassuring squeeze.

"I'm glad I brought along those gifts—the clothes and blankets for the baby. Sherri didn't have anything with her," Felicity murmured.

During the quick drive to the hospital, Felicity had realized that no one was prepared for the baby's arrival. Still, Sherri had seemed calm, even relaxed, and Miles, although concerned, had reacted with his usual competent air. The only truly nervous person had been Felicity, and Seth had made it his personal responsibility to soothe her frazzled nerves. Thank goodness she'd asked him along, she thought, once again checking the time. It was after nine o'clock at night, and passing the tedious wait alone would have been nerve-racking.

"Felicity?" It was Miles, his face aglow, his eyes filled with joy. "We have a girl. An absolutely perfect little girl."

"Oh, Miles!" Felicity sprang from her chair and threw her arms around him. "I'm so happy for you. How's Sherri?"

"She's fine. Just fine. And so is the baby. We've named her Amanda."

Seth rose and extended his hand to Miles. "Congratulations to both of you."

"Thanks. Thanks so much." Miles was grinning from ear to ear. "You can see the baby in a few minutes at the viewing window, and then she goes back to Sherri. They're settling my wife into her room right now."

Felicity reached for her purse. "Do I have time to make a few phone calls to Silverton, Miles? I need to call the hotel there and check out, and have them send my luggage here." *And call Bill and tell him I won't be coming back to work,* she added silently. She avoided Seth's eyes. In spite of her happiness over the new baby, the thought of leaving Seth was agony.

"Felicity..." Miles reached for her arm to stop her exit. "Felicity, would you mind *not* staying with us?"

"What?" Felicity froze in midstride.

"I know Mother wanted someone to stay with us after the baby was born. In fact, she was quite insistent. But Sherri and I just want to be alone with our daughter."

"But I thought you needed help," Felicity said in confusion. "Don't you?"

Miles sat down on the waiting-room couch and gently pulled her next to him. "It's very hard telling your mother you don't want her around for the birth of her grandchild. But you're my sister. I know you'll understand."

Felicity looked up at her brother's face, not trying to hide her bewilderment at his request. "Understand what?"

"This is a very special time for us. You and the rest of the family will have plenty of time later to visit with us and the baby. But right now we'd like to spend it alone. Just me, Sherri and Amanda. Do you mind terribly?"

Felicity looked into Miles's eyes and saw the shining happiness there. She couldn't do anything to mar that, even if she was a little upset. But then she remembered the way Sherri's and Miles's eyes had met in love so many times at the restaurant. They didn't need her around, not really. And she wouldn't have to leave Seth yet. That wasn't bad news at all.

"I understand," she said to Miles. "You give Sherri my love, and kiss the baby for me."

She was rewarded with another radiant smile from her brother. "Thanks, Felicity. I'll give you a call when we get back to the ranger station."

Felicity nodded and gave her brother a final hug.

"Seth, I can trust you to take care of her?" Miles asked.

"You know I will," Seth replied. Miles nodded, and Felicity watched as he left them both without a second glance.

"Are you okay?" Seth asked a few moments later.

Felicity looked up thoughtfully. "They're so very, very happy."

"You helped," Seth said. "Not everyone would understand their wish to be alone together. But then, you're not everyone, are you?"

Felicity didn't know what to say to that. "Let's go see the baby."

"It's a good thing you brought your camera this trip," Seth remarked, tugging her to her feet. "How's it feel to have a new niece?" His voice seemed a shade envious, and Felicity remembered he was an only child.

"Absolutely great, now that awful waiting is over." Hand in hand, they hurried over to the viewing window. "Look, there she is!"

Amanda Barrett was fast asleep, her name written in big bold letters on a pink card above her head.

"Isn't she adorable? Oh, I wish she'd open her eyes!" Felicity gently tapped her nail against the glass.

"She's had a hard first day. Let her sleep." Seth drew her hand away from the glass, and once again, held it lightly in his own.

"Aren't you going to take any pictures?" Seth reminded her, for Felicity remained close to the viewing window, gazing at the delicate new face.

"In a minute." She continued to study the child, and Seth finally removed the camera from her other hand and proceeded to take some shots himself.

Felicity barely noticed the picture-taking, for she was too wrapped up in the strong maternal feelings Amanda had aroused. Suddenly she wanted to feel her own child in her arms, and to see the child's father with the same proud look of joy she had just observed in Miles. She wanted to know that someday her future would hold a family—a family that included Seth.

That realization overwhelmed her. She felt the pull of two different forces, with Portland and her job calling her in one direction, and Seth and Silverton in another. How could she possibly have them both?

"Felicity, didn't you hear me? The nurse said we have to leave. Visiting hours are over."

"Sorry. I wasn't listening." Felicity gave the baby one final glance.

Seth watched her with a strange expression on his face. "That's okay. We really should find a hotel and then get something to eat. We missed dinner, and thanks to Amanda here, we never finished lunch." Seth placed an arm around her shoulders and urged her away from the window. "Come on, we have to go."

He called a cab to take them to a small motel within walking distance of the train station. They stopped at a nearby diner and ordered some soda, barbecued-beef sandwiches and French fries to eat back at the hotel.

"What a wild day," Felicity sighed as she finished the last of her meal and wiped her sticky fingers on a paper napkin. "I started out with a scenic train trip and ended up with a beautiful niece."

Seth tossed the wrappers and napkins in the trash can in his room. "You're very lucky," he said, rejoining her on the bed, where she sat cross-legged for their informal picnic.

Again Felicity heard an envious note in his voice. "I could make you an honorary uncle, if you want. I know you don't have any brothers or sisters," she said lightly.

Seth glanced up in surprise. "I wasn't complaining, although I do appreciate the offer. Today the hospital brought back a lot of memories. I started thinking about my own child..."

His voice trailed off, and it was Felicity's turn to look surprised. "Seth, I didn't know you'd had a child! I'm sorry. I was so happy today for Miles, I didn't even think you might not want to be there."

"It wasn't that at all." Seth sounded odd.

"Would you tell me about it?" Felicity suggested softly.

He shrugged. "It's not much of a story. I always wanted children. I think I told you I designed my house with that in mind. I built extra rooms for kids and made certain the cabin was near safe places for them to play. I really wanted a family."

"And seeing Amanda reminded you of that?"

"Yes." Seth's expression grew wistful. "Having children was about the only thing Valerie and I agreed on. She became pregnant during my last year of college. We were both overjoyed."

The wistfulness changed to sorrow, and Felicity was filled with foreboding. "Seth, what happened?"

There was a slight pause before Seth answered, "After Valerie became pregnant, we decided she should go home and stay with her parents. She'd been living in the dorms with me. Valerie always wanted to go to college herself, but her parents couldn't afford to send her. I had all I could do to support us and pay my own tuition, so I told her I would graduate soon, get a good job, and then send her to school after the baby was born."

"And did she get into school after you graduated?"

Seth shook his head. "Valerie hated being home again with her parents. That's when things started to go bad for us."

Felicity couldn't believe what she was hearing. "Seth, I always assumed you had a happy marriage! You and your wife shared the same background. You should have had so much in common."

"That wasn't the case at all." Seth was silent, and for a moment Felicity thought he wasn't going to say any more. "It wasn't until after she moved home again that I found out Valerie had always hated small-town life. She wanted to move back into the dorms with me. I already had a male roommate by then, and while I tried to make other arrangements for us, Valerie grew more and more restless.''

Felicity's face softened with sympathy. "She left you?"

"Yes." Felicity could see that the admission was painful. "I immediately came back to Silverton when her parents called me. They said Valerie had taken the car and some clothes, and was going to Denver to find a job. They also said she didn't want me going after her."

"But you did?" Knowing Seth, Felicity was certain of that.

"I did. I had to. She was six months pregnant when she left me, and I was worried sick. Not many employers would hire an obviously pregnant woman, and the only job experience Valerie had was waitressing. That's no job for an expectant mother, rushing around on her feet all day. And I honestly thought we could work out our problems."

His face was bleak. "She decided to leave me in the middle of winter. On that day a storm blew up out of nowhere. Felicity, you never saw such snow. And it was so cold. I was dressed for the weather, and I was still freezing."

Felicity's hand crept up to his shoulder.

"The roads were terrible, and Valerie wasn't used to driving in those conditions. I usually did all the driving." He paused a moment, then went on in an echo of his usual voice, "I found Valerie's car before the police did. It had skidded off the side of the road, and fallen down an embankment. Valerie was still alive when I reached her, though how, I'll never know. Her injuries were extensive, but because of the cold and shock, she was more numb than in pain."

Seth swallowed hard. "I flagged down a motorist to get an ambulance, then I went back and put my arms around her. She opened her eyes just once and said, 'I'm sorry.' Then she died."

"Oh, Seth." Tears ran down Felicity's face, but Seth's eyes were dry, still vacantly fixed on the past.

"The baby was too young, and Valerie's injuries too serious, for it to have a chance to live. The doctors didn't even try to deliver the child once they reached the hospital. They said it was hopeless. I never knew if it was a boy or a girl. That bothered me for a long time. I really thought our child should have a name, but how could I give it one?"

Seth's gaze finally focused on Felicity, and he offered her a poignant smile. "Believe it or not, it was Emil who helped. He really stuck by me during the rough times. He suggested I pick out a neutral name for the baby. You know, like Pat or Terry. I did, and that helped. But sometimes, something will happen, like seeing Amanda, and it all comes back like it was yesterday...."

He closed his eyes, hiding their pain-filled depths. "And I wonder about what might have been."

Felicity didn't say a word, but she put her arms around him and silently sent him all the comfort in her heart, hoping to ease his hurt. After a while, Seth straightened. He kissed her lightly on the forehead, now comforting her.

"Don't look so sad, Felicity. You should be celebrating. I shouldn't even have brought it up. It's not a story to hear on your niece's birthday."

"I'm glad you did, Seth. And I'm glad you were with me today." Felicity dried her tears and hugged him again.

"I'm very happy to have met your niece. And I'm even happier that it all went so perfectly for your brother and his wife. Amanda is a beautiful baby." He smiled, letting Felicity know that in spite of the sadness he felt at the loss of his own child, he still shared in the joy of this birth.

"Thank goodness she looks like Sherri and not Miles," Felicity added, trying hard to steady her voice for Seth's sake.

"There's nothing wrong with the Barrett looks," he declared. "I bet you'll have perfectly beautiful children, if you can ever work them into your busy schedule."

"Some day..." Her voice trailed off, and Seth met her gaze intently.

"That day could be whenever you want, with me, Felicity," Seth said quietly.

Felicity's eyes fluttered wide open in shock. She felt a rush of joy, then reminded herself to tread warily. His love was everything she wanted, but she couldn't live in his world. She knew all too well that, for her, the daily dissatisfactions—of being unoccupied, isolated, bored— would wear down their love, no matter how strong.

"I wasn't going to say anything yet, but your brother convinced me otherwise," Seth went on.

"Miles?" Felicity remembered the serious conversation she and Sherri had interrupted during lunch.

"Yes." Seth took both her hands in his. "Miles advised me not to let you go home before I told you how I felt about us. He said that once you were back in Portland, your work would overwhelm you again, and if I wanted to be a part of your life, I should make my bid now."

"Miles said that?" Felicity was astonished by Seth's revelation, and by the thought of Miles talking so intimately to another man on such short acquaintance.

Seth nodded. "Ever since we met, I know you've thought that Silverton's been my primary interest. But it's not. You, on the other hand, obviously consider Portland and Barrett Shipping *your* first priority. I want to come first in your thoughts, Felicity, like you do with me."

"Seth, I care about you very much," Felicity said carefully, still afraid to admit the depth of her feelings. "But I have to go back. I have commitments to my job and to my family. And even if I didn't, what would I do here in Silverton? I need to work!"

Seth's jaw tightened. "I didn't ask you to stay here, did I? That wasn't my question. And Miles did warn me you wouldn't stay away from Portland long. But before you go home, I want to know if we have any kind of future together. I'm not satisfied with merely enjoying the present. I love you! I want to marry you."

He loves me, Felicity's heart repeated. *He loves me!*

"Tell me you feel the same, and you'll make me the happiest man in Colorado."

Felicity's wild elation fought with despair. "I do love you, Seth. I do. But how could I marry you? I can't work here in Silverton. And how can you research your books in Oregon?"

"I'm not interested in the answers to long-term questions right now," was his reply. "I'm only interested in one thing. Will you marry me?"

Felicity couldn't look him in the face. Her chin dropped, and her eyes fixed on his hands. "I don't know. Sometimes I think, yes, I could, because I'll go crazy if I leave you," she agonized. "But then I think that I'll go crazy if I stay in Silverton, with nothing to do. And I tell myself that if I really loved you, my work and my job wouldn't matter so much. But they do, and I can't give it all up, any more than I'd ask you to give up your work for me. There just doesn't seem to be any solution, Seth, and I can't make any promises, no matter how much I love you.''

"So you *do* love me." Seth seemed more satisfied with her jumbled answer than she would have thought possible. "At least there's hope, then." He gave her a look that thrilled her to her very soul. "Time is what we need, Felicity, and we won't have that if you leave for Portland right away. Can't you postpone your departure?''

"I have commitments, Seth. If I don't keep those commitments the company might suffer financially. Couldn't you come to Portland with me for a while?'' she asked hopefully. The thought of actually saying goodbye to him was too painful to contemplate.

"I have to wait until the commercials are safely finished and the results of the uranium survey come in. If there's a large uranium deposit, I don't dare leave Emil alone.''

"And I don't dare leave my company stranded without me.'' Felicity said, her throat tight and dry. "Seth, I'm solely in charge of marketing and sales for Barrett Shipping. My position—what I do—is something that can't be delegated for long. My assistant is filling in for me right now, and he's good, but he's only trained to handle the routine work. The more pressing business matters have to be tabled until I return, and they can only remain pending for so long. Seth, I have to go home. If I don't, Barrett Shipping stands to lose thousands and thousands of dollars.''

They stared sadly at each other.

"I'll write. I'll call. And I'll come back at a later date,'' she promised.

"Will you?" Seth asked. "Or will a few weeks back in the city make your stay here seem dull by comparison? Your memories of us might fade into insignificance."

Felicity blinked to keep back the tears. "They won't, Seth," she whispered.

"But you'll still leave, without even your promise to marry me."

Felicity said nothing, but her mute agony gave Seth his answer. "Well, I can't say I'm surprised. Your brother did warn me." He rose from the bed, the lines of his face looking etched in stone.

Felicity felt sick inside. "Seth, I just can't commit myself to a long-distance marriage. It wouldn't be fair to either of us."

Seth asked one last question. "Are you at least going back to Silverton before you leave?"

Felicity couldn't meet his gaze. "I thought I'd go straight to Portland from here. I'll pick up what I need locally, and send for my other things later." She lifted her head. "But I'd like to see you off in the morning, Seth. Please stop by for me before you leave."

"If that's what you want," he said quietly. "Good night, Felicity."

The next morning came far too soon. She and Seth waited awkwardly for the conductors to allow passengers to board.

"I suppose you'll be happy to see those big-city lights again," Seth said, staring down at his ticket.

"Not as much as you'd think," Felicity admitted miserably. She shifted uneasily from one foot to the other. Goodbyes were always difficult, but this one was tearing her apart.

"When can you come back? Or will you?" Seth asked.

Felicity shifted her feet again. "I will, I promise, but I don't know when I can get away."

Seth's expression revealed little, and Felicity reached into her purse and pulled out her business card, and then her personal one.

"Here," she said, thrusting them at him. "For your Christmas-card list. Don't lose them. My home phone is unlisted."

"I won't." Seth slipped the cards into his wallet. "Would you like mine?"

"I already copied down your address and your home phone number. I know how to reach you."

Seth gave her a ghost of a smile. "Then I'll look forward to hearing from you." He extended his hand. "It's been a . . . pleasure."

Felicity forlornly let him take her hand in his, and then she was tight against his chest, his lips hard on hers for one last kiss.

"I'll miss you terribly," he whispered, his words hoarse in her ear.

"I'll miss you, too." She swallowed hard. "I hope everything works out for Silverton with the commercials and the tourists and all."

Seth slowly released her. He was silent for a moment and he seemed to be choosing his next words carefully.

"I thought," he finally said, his voice bleak, "that you cared enough to stick around and find out. Goodbye, Felicity."

He dropped her hand and then hurried for the train. She knew he didn't hear her parting words, "But I do care, Seth. I really do."

The locomotive shuddered, then with a grinding of metal and a final scream of the whistle, the train carried Seth away. Her heart seemed to shatter into a thousand little pieces, and Felicity realized instantly that she'd made a mistake. Nothing was worth losing Seth. Nothing. How could she have been so blind? She loved him, and she'd let him go.

Ten minutes later she was at a phone, calling for a chartered helicopter. She cared desperately—about him, but about his town, too—and she intended to see that Seth knew it.

The helicopter trip took far less time than the train, bringing Felicity back to Silverton a full hour before Seth. While she was impatient with the wait, it left her time to call her parents and relay the good news about the baby, and then tell them of her change in plans.

"Felicity, I really can't believe that Miles told you to leave," Emily Barrett exclaimed. "Are you sure you heard right?"

"Yes, Mother, I'm sure. He wants to be alone with Sherri and the baby, and it wasn't my place to disagree."

"I don't know what to make of all this, but your brother always did march to the beat of a different drummer. As long as Sherri and Amanda are okay..." Emily's voice trailed off uncertainly.

"They are. I have plenty of pictures, and I'll mail them to you as soon as they're developed.

"Mail them?" Emily was clearly confused. "Aren't you coming home?"

"Not right away. I have some...unfinished business to take care of."

"Business? In Colorado?"

"Yes, very urgent business. In fact, it's a matter of extreme importance. I'll explain everything later. Right now I have to run. My love to everyone. Goodbye."

Felicity firmly rang off despite her mother's protests. She could only hope Emily Barrett would concentrate on

thinking about her first granddaughter. In the meantime, she had to check in with Bill to see if she was still
needed. And then she had to let Seth know she was back
in town. They had a lot to settle before she got on a plane
to go anywhere.

Bill was relieved to see her. The missing costumes still
hadn't turned up, and there were very few women besides Felicity who had complete outfits. Felicity guessed
Emil hadn't yet found a safe moment to return the
clothing undetected.

During her trip to Durango, the commercials at the
mine had been filmed, but not to Bill's satisfaction. The
rain had caused some mud slides at the shooting site, and
the actors had been muddy, miserable and unsure of their
footing. The one good take of the day had been ruined
when a small aircraft had flown across the sky, ruining
the period setting.

Felicity was disturbed to hear that things weren't going
well. Accordingly to Bill, none of the film footage taken
so far was worth much. She knew Seth would be worried
about Emil if Bill's crew decided to stay longer. She also
knew that if the commercials were discarded altogether,
the town stood to lose a good deal of extra merchant
revenue.

So when Bill announced she would be needed for one
last commercial, Felicity breathed a sigh of relief. At least
he was still filming. Maybe this time everything would
proceed without a hitch. After all, Silverton's senior citizens had sworn to be on their best behavior.

Bill planned to shoot a mock train robbery on the D&S
Railroad, complete with men on the train roof. The ef-
fect would be quite dramatic, and Bill expected that this
commercial would highlight the existence of the D&S
railroad much more effectively than just simple scenery

shots would. He explained to Felicity that she'd be a passenger inside the train.

"I'll see you tomorrow morning, Miss Barrett. The usual time. Get into costume, then grab a ride out to the train station. I don't want you walking and getting that costume dirty. We have few enough left as it is."

"You won't be needing me for today, then?" Felicity asked hopefully.

"No. I want to try one more time to reshoot that mine commercial. The footage we have now is a disgrace."

Relieved, Felicity nodded. Then, as soon as Bill had turned his back, she checked her watch. If she hurried, she could get to the station in time to meet Seth, and she was determined to be there.

Sure enough, the train was pulling in just as Felicity was walking briskly down Twelfth Street. She sprinted the rest of the way. Seth was back!

The train braked, with the steam engine screaming and the wheels sending up sparks. Felicity turned her head to protect her eyes from the dirt and soot, then eagerly opened them to look for Seth. She scanned the groups of people dismounting, the tourists obvious with their luggage and camera bags.

There he is, Felicity thought joyfully as she spotted his familiar form stepping down from the third car. It was funny how she could instantly pick him out of a crowd. She hurried closer to the exiting passengers, wanting to touch him, wanting to tell him her news. She tried to call his name, but found she couldn't speak. Instead she waved her arm wildly, hoping to draw his attention.

She did. Seth looked with disinterested eyes toward the motion, then with disbelief. Felicity saw him mouth her name. Instantly his face was transformed, as joy animated every feature, every movement. He started to run, then caught himself. He walked swiftly toward her, threading his way among the milling passengers, every step alive with eagerness.

Felicity quickly wiped the tears from her eyes. She still had to go back to Portland, she warned herself. But she knew that her face reflected his happiness, and the two of them beamed at each other while Seth rapidly closed the distance between them. Then she was in his arms.

"My beautiful Felicity..." Seth spoke first, his pleasure unconcealed from everyone around them. Several strangers glanced their way and smiled. "I thought you were catching a plane to Portland."

"I was, but I want to finish out my film contract first. You know me, the dull, businesslike type. I wouldn't feel right about running out in the middle of a job." She paused, then committed herself. "Besides, I couldn't go home without answering your marriage proposal. My answer, by the way, is yes."

She watched the range of emotions that crossed his face—shock, disbelief, then pure delight. He looked younger, happier, more handsome than she'd ever seen him. His arms tightened, and he gave her another hug that lifted her off her feet and had her gasping for breath. She was finally set back on the ground, but his arms still encircled her.

"Felicity, I can't believe you actually came back. I thought I'd have to follow you to Portland if I wanted to see you again."

"I'll be on the commercials, you know," Felicity reminded him in a shaky voice as they walked away from the station. "Just turn on your TV, and I'll be there in living color."

Seth gave her a rueful look. "That remains to be seen. From what I hear, Bill only has one decent commercial—that's the original saloon-girl scene, and it's not great. But I want to talk about *us*, Felicity. I don't want to talk about the commercials.''

''But Seth,'' Felicity exclaimed with surprise, ''there can't *be* an 'us' until this thing with the commercials is settled. You know that.''

''I don't know that at all. All I know is that you're here with me and not on some plane to Portland. I don't want to hear about commercials, or tourists, or anything that doesn't concern us. Come home with me, Felicity.''

''Home?'' she echoed.

''Yes. My Jeep's parked near your hotel. We can stop at your room and then leave. You don't have to work to-day, do you?''

Felicity shook her head. ''Not until tomorrow morning.''

''We can spend the rest of the day together. We have a lot to discuss.''

Felicity nodded. She and Seth walked to the hotel and she ran in to grab a change of clothes, then hurried back to the Jeep.

The sun was out, and they made the journey to the house in good time, arriving shortly after noon.

''I'll fix you something to eat if you're hungry,'' Seth offered.

''I'm not really, but go ahead and eat if you are,'' Felicity told him. She hadn't eaten any lunch, but food was the last thing on her mind.

''I'd rather just sit and talk.'' He gestured toward the couch, and they both sat down, carefully not touching.

''Why did you come back, Felicity?'' He asked the question straight out, with no preliminaries. ''What made you decide that Portland could wait?''

This was not the time for any more half-truths; Felicity understood that. "I came back because I love you, and I hadn't told you I'd marry you."

Seth's eyes closed, as if he was savoring her words. And when they opened, they were even more brilliant than they'd been when he had seen her at the train station.

"And because I care about this little town," Felicity went on. "This small, isolated, unlikely place in the middle of nowhere has come to mean a great deal to me. I wanted to make sure the commercials got finished, and Silverton continues to thrive, not on uranium finds, but on tourists and old silver mines, just like you want it."

Seth nodded. "I'm very glad, Felicity." His manner became even more serious as he looked her straight in the eyes. "And then?"

"And then I don't know."

"Felicity, I want to marry you! I want us to spend the rest of our lives together. That's going to be a bit difficult with me here in Colorado and you in Oregon. Tell me what you want, what you're feeling."

Felicity thought hard about that. "I wouldn't mind leaving Portland," she said slowly. "It's taken me a long time to realize that. I've never had any reason to leave before. I wouldn't even miss the family business. I've given too much of myself to it—the headaches convinced me of that. It's time for a change, which is what I intend to tell my family. But Seth, I need to work. I'm not a domestic person. I couldn't just play house while you wrote. It would drive me crazy. And then I'd drive *you* crazy."

"You could never do that," Seth scoffed, but Felicity shook her head.

"You're wrong, Seth. I'm a workaholic. I always have been, and I always will be. I've learned my lesson from Barrett Shipping, and I won't ever endanger my health again, but I can't suddenly shift into a life of leisure. I'm good at marketing, and I enjoy the challenge. I don't necessarily need to live near Portland, or even work in the shipping industry, but I do need to live in the city. Someone with my skills could never find a job in a little town like Silverton."

Seth shrugged. "That's no problem. I can move to Portland."

"You...you'd do that for me?" Felicity asked, deeply touched at his sacrifice.

"Why not? I don't intend to have a long-distance marriage. I can write my books anywhere."

"But what about your research?" Felicity still couldn't believe her ears.

"I can always fly back for any research. I'd only need to make one trip a book."

Felicity shook her head. "You're making all this too easy for me."

"Not really. I do still need to wait for the results of that land survey," Seth reminded her. "Once that's in, and the commercials are finished, I can leave."

"I just hope the survey says there isn't any uranium," Felicity remarked. "If there *is*, Seth, will you still want to move to Portland?"

"I see no problem in doing that *and* taking care of my commitments here."

Seth sounded positive, but Felicity wasn't so sure. Certainly everything would be fine if the survey was negative, but how could Seth leave Silverton if it wasn't? Would he resent her for taking him away from a town that needed him? And how would he feel about raising his children in the city? She looked around her at the house he had designed with a family in mind. Did he really love her enough to leave Silverton without a backward glance? She was afraid of hidden resentments that might return to haunt their marriage later. It was a disquieting thought, and it made Felicity uneasy.

"You're worried, aren't you?" Seth asked.

"We haven't known each other for very long. And you're giving up so much..."

"It's not what I'm giving up, Felicity. It's what I'm getting in return. I don't know when it first started to happen for me, but I grew more certain of my love for you every day. And when you were trapped on that runaway stage, I realized I couldn't live without you. So don't worry about trivial things like *where* I live. There comes a time in every man's life when he has to choose what's most important to him. I've made my choice, and I know it's the right one."

Felicity lifted her face to his in wonder. "I thought everything would be so hard to work out. When I saw you leave on that train, I couldn't stand it. It never occurred to me that you'd be willing to come to Portland with me."

"But you still came back," Seth said, one hand gently caressing her cheek.

Felicity nodded, loving his touch. "You said the only thing that mattered was what I was feeling, and the details could be worked out later. I decided to believe you, but I didn't think you'd make everything so easy for me."

Seth gave her a tender look. "You didn't make it easy for me, staying in Durango. By the way, how *did* you get back to Silverton before me?"

"In the biggest, fastest helicopter I could hire. I knew I made a mistake five minutes after the train pulled away with you on it."

"It took you that long?" Seth scolded, but there was no anger in the hand that stroked her hair.

"Some of us are slow learners," Felicity said blissfully. "I didn't think you'd be interested in a big-city businesswoman like me."

"Let me show you how interested I am," Seth proposed.

And when his lips finally left Felicity's she had no doubts at all about his feelings.

She rested her head on Seth's shoulder, her heart soaring. For a long while the two sat in contented silence. Then, sighing deeply, Seth said, "I know you have to work tomorrow. Do you want me to take you back to the hotel now?"

"Are you trying to get rid of me?" Felicity asked playfully.

"I'm working hard at being a gentleman," Seth retorted. "But if you want to stay, I can drive you back early tomorrow morning." He kissed her neck lightly and gave her a slightly wicked grin. "Need a massage?" he asked.

"Only if you're giving it," Felicity whispered. She smiled, a blissful, womanly smile that hinted at the mysteries of love unlocked, and she knew Seth recognized it. As she watched his eyes gleam with desire and with tenderness, the joy deep inside her finally bubbled to the surface and broke all restraints.

"I love you," he murmured as Felicity moved closer into his arms, and then he proceeded to show her exactly how much.

Their coming together was everything they could have wished, and more. There was no uncertainty on either side, and the security they both felt left them free to learn, free to love. When the wonder was over, Felicity lay contentedly in Seth's embrace, feeling that she'd learned more about him in one moment of love than in all the time she had known him.

And although her newfound knowledge gave her joy, it also brought her sadness. She sensed that when Seth made a commitment, it was forever. Seth loved her, but he also loved Silverton. If the uranium survey came back positive, she hoped Silverton's claim on Seth wouldn't be greater than her own.

CHAPTER NINE

"ALL RIGHT, EVERYONE, that was the last rehearsal. This is for real," Bill announced through his megaphone. "Do any of you stunt people need more practice before we start the train?"

Jim and Jesse Colt smiled confidently. They were to play the robbers on the train roof. The other two men who were to play the sheriff and his deputy shook their heads. "We're all set, Bill," Jim yelled.

Felicity was keyed up, as nervous as a first-time actress on opening night. This would be the last commercial, and she was praying for its success. If all went well, maybe Bill would leave Silverton satisfied. Emil and his friends could then be trusted to behave. Seth could come to Portland with an easy conscience. A lot was riding on today.

Long after Seth had fallen asleep with his arms around her last night, Felicity had lain awake imagining the worst scenario—that large deposits of uranium would be found. She could easily imagine Seth trying to fight any government takeover of the town, and she knew for a certainty that he would eventually lose. But that might take years and years, and in the meantime Felicity suspected she would have to take second place in Seth's life. She couldn't imagine him staying in Portland for long under such circumstances. She knew as well as anyone how strong the ties of home could be.

"Okay," Bill called. "All you costumed passengers, board up."

"That's you," Seth said. He gave Felicity a quick kiss and handed her onto the train; they were outside the town, and there was no proper loading platform.

Earlier, on Bill's orders, the engineer had backed the train a few miles out of Silverton. From there the train would slowly approach town, with the climax of the robbery taking place as it pulled into Twelfth Street.

"Thanks," Felicity said, pleased that Seth had finished his consulting duties and followed her into the train. At least she could enjoy a few minutes of his company before the filming started.

"Doesn't the train look perfect?" she asked. The orange-and-black exteriors of the D&S Railroad coaches and their wood-paneled interiors had been washed and polished until they sparkled.

"Yeah, it does. Let's just hope the filming's perfect, too." Seth gave a worried sigh, and Felicity gently traced his chin with her forefinger.

"You aren't expecting more trouble, are you?"

"Felicity, when it comes to these commercials, I expect nothing *but* trouble."

"Surely not your friends?" Felicity lowered her voice, so that none of the other actors could hear.

"No, not them. But I don't know about Bill's two stuntmen. Jim and Jesse could handle being on top of the train blindfolded in the middle of a raging storm, but Bill's employees look awfully nervous. And that makes me nervous."

"Oh, no!"

"Oh, yes. They're an accident looking for a place to happen," Seth predicted.

"Can't you do anything about it?"

"I tried to convince Bill to use just one bad guy and one good guy. That way the Colt brothers could handle things alone, and Bill's stuntmen could stay off the top of the train. But Bill said he wants two of each. Said the arrangements were final." Seth looked gloomily out the window at the rough granite ground below. "It's going to be one painful landing if anyone falls off."

"I'll keep my fingers crossed," Felicity promised.

Seth's forehead furrowed with worry. "At least there's one good thing about all this."

"What's that?"

"You, my love, are safely inside." He brushed his lips across hers, then rubbed at the heavy stage lipstick that had transferred itself to him. "I've got to run, but I'll be back. Bill's going to let me change into costume and join the rest of you actors on the train. I told him I want to make sure everything is historically accurate, but I really want to keep an eye on his stuntmen. In the meantime, try to stay out of trouble, okay? I'd like to see us make it to the altar in one piece."

Felicity smiled. "We could always get married on the train," she suggested.

"Please, I have enough worries with this production," Seth groaned, but Felicity's quip erased some of the tension on his face.

"See you in a few minutes," she said.

"Right." Then he was gone.

Felicity watched through her window as Seth went to change, then she took her assigned seat, carefully spreading the voluminous folds of her long skirt. She was in the second passenger car, while the "good guy" stunt actors were in the first car.

Seth had told her earlier that Bill would be riding on the camera car, a motorized, open vehicle that would run ahead of the train on the same tracks as the D&S. Other stationary camera crews would be strategically positioned beside the tracks.

Immediately after Seth boarded, the short blast of the steam whistle signaled the other actors and actresses to take their places, and the train jerked and pulled until it established a smooth, even rhythm. Up ahead in the camera car the crew filmed the action, adjusting their cameras to the motion of the train and their own vehicle.

"You look great!" Felicity studied Seth's clothes, a well-made reproduction of a gentleman's traveling suit.

Seth grabbed the brim of his matching hat and removed it with a sweeping flourish. "Thanks, although I could do without this." He lightly touched the edge of the handlebar mustache.

"I think it's kind of cute," Felicity said.

"The glue itches like crazy, but the makeup artist insisted. Since I was definitely coming on this trip, I had to give in." He wrinkled his upper lip, causing the waxed ends of the mustache to sway.

"Have you ever acted before?" Felicity asked.

"I help the Colts out from time to time during the summer. That's why the costume fits so well. It's the town's, not Bill's, and was made especially for me. I play a gentleman gambler."

Bill gave the signal, and the train picked up speed. Seth sat down beside her. "We'd better stop talking and start acting."

Felicity nodded, watching out the window for her cue. Sure enough, a few minutes later, Jesse and Jim galloped into sight on their horses. Felicity pretended to cringe in terror when the "outlaws," their faces hidden by bandannas, rode closer to the train and prepared to jump. The ends of the passenger cars had metal safety rails around the tiny platforms, and the brothers aimed their horses toward those.

Felicity, Seth and their fellow passengers crowded over to the windows in pretended horror as the horses, specially trained for stunt work, kept pace with the train. Seth drew a mock pistol from within his waistcoat, and some of the other men readied themselves to "defend" the women.

Jim jumped for the railing first, and Felicity wasn't acting as she held her breath. She exhaled with relief when Jim successfully negotiated the distance and stood up, extending a hand to his brother. Jesse also jumped safely to join him. Then the two horses veered away from the train.

The two men quickly climbed to the roof, and Felicity could hear their steps overhead as they made their way to the front of the train.

"Why are they going on the roof, anyway?" Felicity asked Seth, knowing she could break character, since all the cameras were now focused on the villains.

"The train safes were usually kept in the first car behind the locomotive," Seth explained. "That's where the Colts are headed. From the roof, a train robber could successfully break through the glass and throw a stick of dynamite into the car. There was no safety glass in those days. The men assigned as guards wouldn't have a chance."

"And then what?" Felicity asked.

"Well, the only defense was for the guards to go up on the roof themselves before the robbers reached them in the front car. This is where Bill's two stuntmen come in. They're playing the guards, and they'll go up on the train roof to fight it out with the Colts."

Seth watched closely from the window as the two guards safely negotiated the outside climb to the train roof. Felicity craned her neck, trying to see, but once the actors reached the roof, they were no longer visible. Even though she knew the train was going as slow as possible, the scenery still seemed to be speeding by at an alarming rate.

She could hear the Colt brothers' movements above her, and if they were following the script, the two outlaws had now spotted the guards.

"According to Bill's plan, the guards will shoot blanks at the Colts," Seth explained. "They'll fall off the moving train at a prearranged point, landing on stunt mattresses. Then the guards will climb back inside the car with the safe, and if everything goes right, we'll roll triumphantly into Silverton."

Felicity nodded and readied herself, knowing that she and the rest of the passengers were supposed to act startled as the outlaws' "dead" bodies came tumbling down in front of the passenger windows. The sounds of scuffling could be heard from above, and still Felicity waited.

"Seth, where are the gunshots? Shouldn't we have heard them long before now?"

"Damn!" Seth swore. "If there's much more of a delay, the Colts will overshoot the safety mattress."

"What's taking so long?" one of the other costumed actors mumbled.

Felicity's hands splayed against the window as she twisted her neck and tried to see above her. The scuffling sounds increased. Then, finally, someone rolled off the roof and fell.

One of the women next to her screamed, and Felicity felt the scream echo inside her head as her stomach lurched in horror. The man who fell wasn't one of the

Colt brothers. It was one of the guards, and he hadn't fallen anywhere near the stunt mattress. Felicity immediately reached for the emergency-stop wire above her head, but Seth had already pulled it. The pride of the Durango & Silverton Railroad jerked to a screeching halt.

The next few minutes were pure pandemonium. Seth was the first one off the train. Everyone else exited, and costumed and street-clothed people raced to cover the distance to the fallen man. Felicity struggled to follow, but the heavy skirts on her period dress slowed her down. Seth ran ahead, and he reached the fallen guard just in time to see him stand up, brush himself off and gingerly touch his face.

"I think I lost a tooth," was all he said.

The emergency medics pushed their way through the crowd and examined him. Miraculously, a cut lip and a missing tooth seemed to be the man's only injuries. He'd plunged onto a long-dead, uprooted pine tree, and the massive pile of decaying vegetation had broken his fall.

Felicity caught up to Seth, and threw her arms around him. Her legs were wobbly with relief. Had it not been for a rotting tree, she would have seen a man die an ugly death.

Bill finally made it through the crowd, accompanied by another man Felicity didn't recognize. Bill looked at his stuntman in amazement. "You're okay?" he asked incredulously.

"He'll be fine," the medics assured him before leading the man away.

"Now what?" one of the other actors asked. "Are we going for another take today?"

Felicity shifted in Seth's arms until they were standing side by side. She honestly didn't think she was up to another performance. How could she act after her terror of the past few minutes on the train?

The man next to Bill shook his head gravely, then walked away.

Bill's shoulders sagged. "That was our insurance man, ladies and gentleman. He's just canceled coverage of this project. That means no more commercials and no more filming. Please get back on the train for the ride into town, and then you can all collect your paychecks. This project is officially scrapped."

The arm around Felicity's shoulder went rigid, and Felicity gazed up at Seth in dismay. "Seth, he can't do that, can he?"

"It looks like he just did. Damn! All those jobs Bill provided just ended! And we won't be getting that television exposure the merchants were counting on, either."

Felicity tried to console him. "It was an accident, Seth," she said. "And Bill couldn't have provided much more work anyway. This was supposed to be the last commercial. Maybe it's all for the best. At least now Emil won't have to worry about more tourists on his land discovering the you-know-what?"

"Maybe you're right." Seth brightened a little, but they both quickly changed their opinion at Bill's next words.

"Listen up, everyone! When you come to collect your pay, I want the names and addresses of anyone here who's interested in working on remakes of these commercials. I'm going to have the insurance investigators check out the problems we've been having. If foul play is proven, and I suspect it will be, the insurance company has to pay up and we're back in business. If you're interested, let me know."

Bill's face clearly showed that he had no doubts about returning, and Felicity's heart sank at the news. "Seth," she said with dismay, "what if the investigators find the—"

"Not another word, Felicity." Seth abruptly cut her off. "It's too crowded here to talk. Just get on the train."

"But what about—"

Seth shook his head, then took her arm and guided her back to the train. "Later, Felicity. Now let me think."

As the train slowly made its way back to Twelfth Street, the passengers were deathly quiet. The other walk-ons were glum and disappointed, while the regular staff actors murmured about Bill's anger, and how the government stood to lose a great deal of money by funding the useless commercials. Felicity's spirits sank even lower as she heard one man knowledgeably report that Bill had suspected sabotage for some time and intended to prove it. That way, the government would be reimbursed by the insurance company. And Bill wouldn't have to suffer any retribution from his superiors.

She glanced over at Seth, beside her on the seat, wondering what he thought about that. But he seemed lost in thought, and Felicity knew better than to disturb him. How could the town keep the discovery of the uranium a secret from professional investigators? It was bound to get out. After all, she had learned the whole story in less than two weeks.

The train pulled to a stop with a screech and a shudder.

"Wait for me in the bar at the hotel after you change," Seth ordered. "I'm going to get changed, then see if the results of the survey are in yet. I'll meet you there as soon as I can."

As Felicity changed for the last time in the wardrobe building, she prayed Seth wouldn't be too long. Even if the survey showed little uranium, that still didn't solve the problem of the lost television exposure for the tourist town. How in the world could Seth fix this? To make things worse, Felicity knew in her heart that she couldn't ask him to leave Silverton with these issues unresolved.

Felicity hung up the brocade, then put on her own clothes. She gave the stage makeup a quick swipe, let the curls of her period hairstyle remain and raced over to the hotel.

She entered the Grand Imperial, then hurried to the hotel's Hub Saloon. The moment she stepped into the dim room with its old, pressed-tin ceiling, she saw Seth.

"Did you find out anything?" she asked breathlessly as she took a seat next to him at the huge bar.

"Not yet. My friend's over the flu, but he's still at Emil's. We should know the results later today. Would you like something to drink? After a train ride like the one we just had, I think we deserve it."

"No, nothing for me. Seth, what are we going to do? If Bill's looking for a scapegoat, we both know he won't have far to look. Emil's as good as jailed, and everyone will know about the uranium!"

Seth signaled the bartender, ordering a scotch. "The jury's still out on the uranium," he said, "but I wouldn't like to see anyone in jail. Especially since you had such an obvious part in ruining the commercials yourself. I don't fancy having my wife behind bars."

"I don't think that's funny!"

"Neither do I, Felicity. Believe me, neither do I. Sure you wouldn't like a drink?"

"No! It's going to take more than a drink to set this mess right." Felicity's voice cracked as she fought to combat the fear in her heart. If Seth was going to fight the uranium mining, there would be no place for her in his life.

"Make that two scotches," he said to the bartender. "You need it. Felicity, try not to worry so much."

"That's easier said than done," she muttered. This crisis just meant another delay in their departure for Portland. She took a sip of the drink and choked.

"Smaller sips," Seth warned. "Do you know the history of this bar?" he asked, the question coming out of nowhere.

Felicity sighed. "No, I don't."

"This bar was huge by yesterday's standards, let alone today's. It's custom-made of cherrywood with scrimshaw paneling, and came around the Horn in a sailing ship. It was hauled to Silverton first by train, then by covered wagon."

He took a sip of his scotch. "If you look at that paneling over there, you'll see a bullet hole."

"I see it," she said.

"Well, in Silverton's boom-town days, there was a popular woman named Rosie Steward. She was known as a party girl then, and had lots of suitors. One day a jealous suitor fired off a shot here. Fortunately for Rosie, the bullet ended up in the bar instead of in her."

Felicity saw no connection between this anecdote and their own predicament. "And the moral of the story?"

"Things never went the way people wanted back then, so why should we expect them to go the way we want now? Silverton is full of surprises, and the town's weathered them before. It probably will again. Felicity, much as I hate to admit this, I've decided not to fight the government if the uranium turns out to be a major deposit."

"What?" Felicity cried, unable to believe her ears.

"I don't mean that I'm going to let them take over our town," Seth qualified. "I intend to make certain that, whenever possible, the town's welfare comes first. But I'm not going to take a stand dead against development. It would be useless in the end, and I think Silverton would have better bargaining power with the government if we work with them right from the start. Perhaps if I try to convince Emil and his friends to fight for whatever benefits they want, instead of continuing a hopeless battle, there'll be much less grief for everyone. The uranium mining might be inevitable, but that doesn't mean we have to throw in the towel altogether."

To Felicity, this meant only one thing. "You'd be staying on in Silverton, then?"

"Yes. This will delay my move to Portland, but not for long," he emphasized. "I want to make sure all our residents use their energies for constructive, not destructive, purposes. We've had enough of that already."

Deep relief swept through Felicity. "I'm glad you feel that way, Seth. You'd have more of a say in Silverton's future by working with the government than by opposing them hands down."

"I agree, no matter how much I'd like things to remain the same. Compromise is better than having no say at all."

"But what about the insurance investigation and the unfinished commercials?" Felicity asked. "I don't want to see your friends in jail. Or me, either, for that matter. And I know you want extra exposure for the tourists for next summer."

"I was thinking about that on the train," Seth admitted, "and it seems to me the main problem Bill has with the commercials is the fact that the real world kept popping onto his film. You're the marketing expert, Felicity. If you could think of some way to salvage that film with the ruined takes, we might be able to keep those insurance investigators out of Silverton."

Felicity's eyebrows knotted in confusion. "I don't know, Seth. I could probably come up with something, but there isn't much time left before Bill leaves."

For the first time some of Seth's anxiety showed. "Come on, Felicity. You're our last chance to salvage these commercials!"

"I'll do my best." Felicity concentrated, mentally reviewing her stay in Silverton and her participation in the commercials. There had to be some way to help Seth. Suddenly an idea flashed through her mind. The business logic that had been part of her all her life started working, analyzing, calculating. Her face took on a look of surprise. Why, it just might work!

"What is it?" Seth asked, watching her closely. "Have you thought of something?"

Felicity pushed away her drink and grabbed his hand. "Maybe I have. Come on, we have to find Bill. I have an idea."

Bill wasn't hard to locate. He was at the D&S platform supervising the loading of the camera equipment. There was no doubt about it. The production company was moving out.

"Bill?" Felicity's greeting was tentative, for Bill was obviously in a foul mood.

"Your paychecks will be ready by tomorrow morning when I leave," Bill said irritably. "Now go away."

"We're not here for our paychecks," Seth announced. "We're here about the commercials."

"There *are* no more commercials, or haven't you been paying attention?"

"There *can* be, if you'll give me five minutes of your time," Felicity said eagerly. "Marketing is my specialty. Seth can confirm that."

Bill looked up, registering Felicity's confidence. "Is she telling the truth?" he asked suspiciously.

Seth nodded. "She is. From what I know, I'd give her a chance to talk."

Bill hesitated, then gave in. "All right, I'll listen. I'm not looking forward to going back to Denver and being chewed out by my boss." He glanced around for his assistant to no avail. "I can't leave the loading of the equipment unsupervised, but go ahead."

Felicity's eyes sparkled with excitement. "You don't have to scrap the commercials. You've got everything on film right now that you need for a successful ad campaign."

Bill snorted derisively. "Sure I do. I have airplanes in my mine commercial, Jeeps driving next to my stagecoach, and modern-day medics in my train commercial. That isn't even including the tennis balls. I hardly think those takes are worth the film they're printed on."

"But they are!" Felicity insisted. "All you have to do is change the slant of your campaign. Right now you're concentrating on the Silverton of yesterday. Try changing your campaign to this—Silverton . . . Is it yesterday or today?"

Bill's eyes narrowed skeptically, and Felicity hurried to explain.

"What's affected me most about Silverton is how the past and the present exist side by side. Hotels from yesterday still operate today. Trains of yesterday still carry passengers. Mines from a hundred years ago are still being worked. Show that in your commercials! Let your television viewers see that Silverton isn't a ghost town just reenacting its past. Silverton's past continues to live in Silverton's present!''

"I could leave in the Jeep rescue with the stage-coach," Bill said slowly.

Felicity nodded excitedly. "Exactly."

"You could leave the plane in the mining commercial, too, and the first-aid treatment of the train guard by the medic," Seth added.

"There's still the ruined shoot-out scene," Bill remarked, but Felicity waved away his objection.

"That's nothing, Bill. All you have to refilm is the part where Jesse rolls off the roof. Have him fall into a crowd of modern bystanders instead of costumed actors, and it will fit the new advertising angle."

"Silverton…is it yesterday or today?" Bill mused. "It just might work."

"Of course it will," Felicity urged, feeling a rising sense of excitement.

"Bill, you could refilm the shoot-out this afternoon," Seth put in. "You'd only need Jesse Colt to roll off the roof. I know he'd do it for you. And he's covered by his own insurance as a stuntman here in Silverton, so you wouldn't have to worry about your own canceled coverage. It would all be perfectly legitimate."

Bill nodded in satisfaction, and Felicity hammered her point home. "Why bother with insurance investigators? You know how these small towns are. They all clam up when it comes to strangers," she said logically, knowing that Seth would forgive her unflattering remark. "You'll just be wasting your money."

"That's the last thing I need," Bill groaned. He paused just a second, then made up his mind. "I think I can pull it off. Seth, can you find Jesse Colt for me and see if he's willing?"

"I'll find him, and I'll be right back," Seth promised. "Are you coming, Felicity?"

"I'd like to talk to Felicity a while longer," Bill insisted. Seth nodded, then turned to hurry toward his Jeep, but not before throwing Felicity a look of shared triumph.

Bill listened to Felicity's suggestions for a few more minutes. Then, "Who are you, Felicity Barrett?" he finally asked.

Felicity pulled out one of her business cards and gave it to him to read.

"President of marketing and sales? You hold *this* position with Barrett Shipping, and you're working as a walk-on actress?" Bill was incredulous.

"It's a long story," Felicity smiled. "But rest assured, I'm not interested in a career as an actress."

"It's a good thing," was Bill's blunt reply. "I'd hate for you to quit your present job because of any false illusions. You did a fair job for a beginner, but I don't ever expect to see you up on the silver screen in a starring role."

Felicity laughed. "That's okay. I never wanted to be there in the first place."

Bill gave her a shrewd look. "What *do* you want, Miss Barrett? You've done me a big favor, and you and I know that most favors cost."

Felicity airily waved her hand. "It's on the house."

Bill wasn't satisfied. "Come on, now. Nothing is free these days. What do you want? Money? Contacts? What?"

"Well...there is something," Felicity said after a few moments' thought. "I kind of like it here in Colorado. If I decide to stay and look around for a job in Denver, could I possibly use your name as a reference?"

"That's all you want?"

"Yes. Maybe I can find employment in the city. Seth and I..." She blushed slightly, her voice trailing off, and Bill smiled with sudden understanding.

"I see." He pulled out his own business card and handed it to her. "I think I can promise you a glowing recommendation."

"Thank you. I really appreciate that."

She carefully pocketed the card, then turned at the sound of Seth's Jeep. Seth and the Colt brothers were inside. Behind the Jeep were numerous other vehicles. It looked as if the entire town had arrived at the station.

"We're back, with plenty of people for you to use as bystanders," Seth happily announced. "And they've all agreed to work without a fee."

"Great!" Bill glanced at his watch, then started shouting orders at his crew. "Get those cameras back to Blair Street! We have time for just one take, and I want to get it right! Felicity, do you want to be part of the crowd?"

Felicity looked questioningly at Seth, who placed his arm around her waist and drew her close.

"Sorry, Bill. The rest of these people are yours, but when it comes to Felicity, I don't intend to share."

Bill gave them both a benevolent smile. "In this case, I quite understand."

CHAPTER TEN

POP! The champagne cork shot out from the bottle, and white foam sprayed onto the top of the cherrywood bar. All the seats at the Imperial's Hub Saloon were filled by town residents. When the shooting of the last commercial was finally finished to Bill's satisfaction, everyone had stopped to celebrate. The television commercials promised a bumper crop of tourists next year, which was certainly a reason to rejoice. And of course, there were the select few who felt very relieved that no insurance investigators would be coming to town, and they celebrated harder than anyone else. The bar was filled with riotous people.

Felicity couldn't quite take it all in, but that didn't matter. She sat quietly, taking pleasure from watching a relaxed, smiling Seth, and greeting all the people who came up to talk to her. It was too bad she wouldn't get a chance to know them all, she thought with regret. She felt a very real part of this community now. But she had a future with Seth to look forward to. She still had to talk to her parents and tell them she was bringing home someone special for them to meet. Baby Amanda wouldn't be the only new member of the Barrett clan.

"Seth, I need to go up to my room for a few minutes. Do you mind?" she asked, her mouth near his ear so she could be heard over the noise.

"I'll come with you." He immediately set down his glass of champagne and made to follow her.

"No, that's okay. You stay with your friends. I want to call home and tell them the good news."

"I wish I could give you a departure date, but I don't know when I can leave. The news from the survey is still pending."

"That's okay," she said, kissing him on the cheek. "I'll tell my parents we'll be home as soon as we can."

Slowly she threaded her way through the crowd, accepting good wishes and smiles from all. She'd almost reached the door when Emil and his friends stopped her.

"Thanks for your help, Miss," he said, and his friends echoed the sentiment. "Seth tells me that if it wasn't for you, the commercials would've been scrapped."

"You're welcome." She gave them a polite smile, waiting for them to step aside so she could go to her room.

"We're all sorry about the trouble we caused, especially about the stagecoach. We never meant any harm."

"I know." She looked at the men, part of Silverton's past. What had Seth said? Silverton was full of surprises, and these four had given her a fair share. They had also given her Seth. If she hadn't noticed them with their dogs after the saloon-girl commercial and told Seth about it, the two of them might not have progressed past that unfavorable first impression. Felicity shivered at the thought.

"You did what you believed was right. I can understand that," she said sincerely.

"You really mean it?"

"I certainly do." She solemnly shook hands with each of them. "Make sure Seth has your addresses so I can invite all of you to our wedding."

The men registered astonishment, and then Emil found his voice again. "Congratulations. And thank you, Miss. You're a real lady."

Felicity smiled, as she went up to her room. She picked up the phone, then hesitated. She didn't have an arrival date to tell her parents, and she wouldn't until she heard the outcome of the uranium survey. If it came back positive, could she really hold Seth to his promise to leave right away? His friends and his home meant so much to him.

Felicity suddenly thought of Miles and Sherri, living happily in the isolation of the mountains. At the hospital, she'd seen how Sherri and Amanda had rightfully replaced parents and family as Miles's first priority. And Miles wouldn't have reaped love's rewards if he hadn't had the courage to put his old life behind him. Seth had promised to do the same for Felicity. If others could be that secure in their love, why couldn't she?

Gently Felicity replaced the receiver. She wasn't being *forced* to give up anything, but she could *choose* to put Portland behind her. Suddenly she was sure the rewards would be great. The new life with Seth right here in Colorado would far outstrip the old. She had made more new friends during one visit to Silverton than she had during the last ten years in Portland. And she could always find another job. Perhaps Denver was the place for her to start. Marketing was her field; there had to be a need for her skills somewhere.

There was a quick knock on the door, then Seth poked his head into the room. "You took so long I started to worry," he said as he came in. "Is everything okay at home?"

"I haven't called yet. Your friends stopped to talk to me—" she began, but Seth interrupted.

"I know. They talked to me, too. I have something to tell you," he said with a grin of anticipation.

"So do I," Felicity announced.

They both spoke at the same moment. "The uranium survey came back negative"..."I'm not going back to Portland."

"What did you say?" they demanded in unison.

Seth took Felicity's shoulders and pulled her down onto the bed. "You first," he ordered.

"I said I'm not going back to Portland. I still intend to work, but I'm giving up the family business."

Seth's face was full of amazement. "But the survey came back negative! My friend said there's just a tiny pocket of extremely low-grade ore here. There's nothing for the government to be interested in, even if they do find out about it. Emil doesn't have to worry about nosy tourists playing prospector on his land."

"There's nothing to find? Are you sure?" Felicity asked excitedly. She felt as though a huge boulder had been lifted from her heart.

Seth nodded. "I can leave for Portland whenever you want."

"But Seth, I don't want to leave, after all. I've changed my mind. I like it here. I think I can be happy here."

"Felicity—" Seth's face revealed disbelief "—I promised you I'd move to Portland. I know how important your work is to you."

"My work is important, but the specific employer isn't. I'll find something else. I'm ready to leave Barrett Shipping. I remember growing up in Portland, Seth. My brothers and I used the company hallways and offices as our playground. The only people I knew were people who worked for my father. I don't want my children to grow up like I did." Felicity thought about the home Seth had built with such care. "I want them to have more than that. And I may be able to work out of Denver. So you see, Silverton's the right choice for us all."

Seth pulled her onto his lap. "Are you sure, Felicity? What about your family?"

"I'll have you," Felicity said tenderly. "And Miles and Sherri aren't far away, either. As for everyone else, they'll have to accept the fact that I'm resigning and staying with the man I love." She felt a sense of freedom, of release, as if she had kicked off a pair of tight shoes.

"Are you now?" Seth asked with a satisfied gleam in his eyes.

Felicity smiled happily. "Better kiss me so I can make sure," she invited—an invitation he immediately accepted.

When she finally came up for air, her eyes sparkled, her hair was tousled, and her lips tingled. "Seth—" she laughed breathlessly "—if you do that again, not only will I never leave Silverton, but I may never get out of this hotel room."

"I can think of worse prospects," Seth murmured. He was just about to take more serious action when another knock sounded at the door. Seth swore as Felicity sat up.

"Who can that be?" she wondered, trying to smooth her hair and straighten her clothes at the same time.

"Whoever it is, they have rotten timing," Seth said.

Felicity silently agreed, but opened the door anyway. It was Bill.

"May I come in, Felicity?" he asked. "I wanted to talk to you before you head back to the party."

"I can spare a few minutes. Come on in." She took a seat on the edge of the bed and gestured Bill toward the Victorian chair.

Bill saw Seth, who didn't look pleased at the interruption. "Hi, Seth. I won't keep Felicity long, so feel free to stay," Bill said before addressing Felicity.

"I checked out your credentials and talked to your brother Roger at Barrett Shipping. It seems you are who you say. I also," he continued, "checked with my boss in Denver. I told him how you saw the obvious solution that the rest of us missed. He wanted me to offer you a job in our marketing department, Felicity."

"A job?" She couldn't believe this was happening. "But—"

"Hear me out. You probably aren't interested, but my boss insisted I talk to you anyway. I know the government doesn't pay as well as private industry, and you'd probably have to take a cut in pay. We can't offer you the salary you're making now, but then, the tourism industry isn't anything like the shipping industry."

"No, it's not," Felicity managed to say.

"However, the marketing principles are the same. Felicity, we need people with fresh ideas, people who can provide original ways to sell our state to tourists. I think that with a little training at our Denver offices, you could be just as good as, if not better than, any of the people we have now. Including me," he added ruefully. "I couldn't come up with the solution to these commercials. Will you please think it over?"

"I . . ." Felicity swallowed and started again. "How long would I have to train in Denver before I could actually get down to work?"

"Four weeks. Six at the most," Bill said eagerly, sensing her interest. "And then you'd be free to develop your marketing campaigns for Colorado's historic and scenic areas. There'd be some traveling, of course. You'd have to become acquainted with each area."

Felicity couldn't believe her incredible good fortune and saw that Seth was just as excited. He did similar traveling when he researched the backgrounds for his books, so could easily arrange his schedule to match hers.

"And when I'm not traveling?" she quickly asked. "Where would I be?"

"You'd be doing most of your marketing development on your own. Of course, you'd have to check in with us three or four times a month, but you could do most of your work at home, and download it over the phone to our offices in Denver. A lot of our staff work from computers out of their homes. We find it very satisfactory for both sides."

"And the pay?" she asked in her most businesslike voice. She had already decided to take the job regardless of salary, but business was business.

Bill named a very reasonable figure. "You'd be eligible for promotions in no time. Are you interested?"

"I believe I am, Bill."

"Great!" He shook her hand, then wrote down a name, address and number for her. "That's my boss. You'll have to arrange an interview with him, but that's just a formality. He wants to meet you and arrange your training as soon as possible—maybe in a month."

"That will be fine." Felicity barely managed to restrain her excitement as she tightly grasped the paper. "I'll look forward to seeing you again."

"As long as it isn't in costume in one of my commercials." He grinned. "I've got to go. Give me a call when you get to Denver."

"Goodbye, Bill. And thank you."

Felicity shook his hand, showed him out, then weakly sat back on the bed.

"Congratulations!" Seth's face mirrored her own joy. "You've just been offered the perfect job."

"I can't believe it. We can stay in Silverton!" She shook her head, marveling. If she hadn't cared enough about Seth and about what happened to the town, she would never have been offered this prize. This isolated place in the middle of the mountains had given her a new job, a new home, and most important, most precious of all, love.

Another knock sounded at the door. "Seth, when are you coming back to the party?" Flo yelled.

"Go on, I'll see you later," Seth yelled back before Felicity even made it to the door. "Come on, Felicity, let's go, or we'll end up with the party in here."

Seth locked the door behind them, then contentedly linked his arm with Felicity's as he headed for the exit leading outside.

"Aren't we going back to the bar?" Felicity asked with surprise.

"I've had enough of that kind of celebrating. Why don't we go back to my place? We can be alone, just the two of us."

"I'd like that," Felicity happily agreed. "Seth, do we have enough light left to walk?" she suggested. "I don't feel like driving."

Seth checked the position of the sun, drifting ever lower in the sky. "The sun won't set for over an hour yet. That's plenty of time."

They started out of town at an easy pace, hand in hand, enjoying a contented silence. It wasn't until they were on the faintly marked trail to Seth's home that Felicity spoke. "I love the quiet."

"I hope you won't miss Portland too much," he said. "The wind rushing in the pines is pleasant enough, but it can get awfully dull to some."

"It won't. Not if we're together," Felicity said with simple logic.

They walked on, Seth helping her over the rocky bottom of a dried stream bed before he said, "With all the excitement from the survey results and the party, I never got a chance to thank you properly for making things right with Bill. If a team of investigators had been assigned to look for evidence of sabotage, I hate to think what would have happened to Emil and the others."

"But nothing happened," Felicity reminded him. "Besides, it was your idea to use the existing film footage of the commercials. I only came up with a way to market it."

"For which I'm very grateful." He pulled her close and kissed her hungrily. To Felicity's delight, passion far outweighed any trace of gratitude in the embrace.

"At least no one can knock on the door and interrupt us here," Seth observed as they moved forward on the trail again.

"Bill I can forgive. After all, he did come to the door with a job offer in hand."

They passed under a canopy of aspens. "True, although I think I'll miss my saloon girl."

Felicity smiled at the amusement in his voice. "Not me. No more indecent dresses and dangerously high heels."

"Pity." Seth sighed with mock disappointment. "I'll have to settle for the real Felicity Barrett instead." His eyes glowed, fiercely possessive. "You'll have to call your family and let them know."

"That's right!" Felicity remembered. "Sherri and Miles will be so surprised!"

"Perhaps not as surprised as you might think," Seth said, not hiding the satisfaction in his voice. "I already asked Miles if he'd be my best man."

"Seth!"

"And if your parents are coming out to see the baby, we could get married then," Seth suggested with a confidence that showed Felicity he had never intended to take no for an answer.

"I'd like them to be here for our wedding," she admitted, "although it will come as a shock to my father. I'll have to fly home soon to finish training my assistant to replace me. Did I ever tell you he's another Barrett? He's a distant cousin who's been waiting for a chance like this for ages. I'll bet I can train him in half the time it would normally take with someone else."

"Then he and I will both be happy when you leave Portland."

Felicity knew Seth was thinking of the time they would have to spend apart. "I owe it to Father and the company, Seth. I'll make sure that's taken care of before I start to work for Bill's people."

"Just make sure you leave us plenty of time for a long honeymoon," Seth warned. "I have a feeling that once you start your new job, I'll be living with a human dynamo."

"I promise not to become a workaholic again. At least I'll try," she added as she saw Seth's skeptical look. "You know, I was thinking...maybe later, when I'm established in my job, we can try to sell some of your nonfiction manuscripts. I know that visitors to historical sites would rather read history written your way than some dry pamphlet. Perhaps we can even get some of your stories onto film or video.''

Seth considered the prospect. "That would be something I'd enjoy working on. History needs to be brought alive. But right now I'm more concerned with the present. Are you positive you want to stay, Felicity? It's all very well to consider living here now, when the leaves are green and the sun is out. But come winter, there's just the cold and the snow and the mountains.''

"There will be us, Seth. That's more than enough.''

The light started to take on an orange tint as the sun's lower edge touched the tops of the western peaks.

"When you first arrived, all you talked about was progress and development for Silverton. What made you change your mind?'' Seth asked as he brushed away a leaf caught in her hair.

"You did, of course. One of your books was the turning point for me.''

"*Tarnished Dreams*?''

"Yes. There was a sense of hopelessness through it all that really made me think twice about Silverton's future. Seth, did you know about the uranium when you wrote it?''

"Unfortunately, yes,'' Seth admitted. "And it shows in the book. I usually don't write such depressing stuff. I like my stories to end happily.''

"Well, real life turned out better than fiction this time.''

They stepped around a fallen tree and back onto the trail.

"For now. But maybe some day something else will happen to change Silverton. The silver and gold were discovered here a hundred years ago, so I suppose that eventually other mineral deposits might be found, too.

These mountains are full of treasures, and where there are treasures, there are bound to be treasure-hunters. I ought to know. I found the most valuable prize of all.'' His voice was rough with emotion as his eyes met hers.

"I realize now that one man can't stop the tide of progress. Much as I would hate a large lode of uranium actually existing, I would accept it and help make the transition a smooth one for Silverton.''

Felicity knew that admission was hard for Seth, and she loved him even more for it.

"I owe this town and its people a lot,'' he went on. "I could never turn my back on them, but if it ever comes down to a choice between them and you, Felicity, you'll always be first. Silverton is my home, but you are my heart.''

They both stopped walking then, and Seth hugged her tightly and sealed his promise with a kiss. Felicity silently vowed that as long as it was within her power, Seth would never be forced to choose. Her final fears about Seth's ties to Silverton dissolved, leaving her soul free to soar.

Tears sprang into her eyes. If she hadn't had those headaches at work, if her sister-in-law hadn't been expecting a baby, if her mother hadn't sent her to Silverton instead . . . She'd been drawn to Seth by a delicately spun web of choices and events, a web that could easily have been torn. But love had provided strength, and the delicate strands of fate that brought them together had now become unbreakable bonds.

"Hey, you're crying!'' Seth was actually surprised.

"I'm just happy,'' Felicity insisted. She wiped her eyes, then tugged at Seth's hand. "Come on, it's getting dark.''

"We're not far,'' Seth assured her. "If we hurry, we can watch the sunset from the house.''

Minutes later the two of them were standing on the porch. The sun flooded the tips of the trees and the rocky peaks with vivid shades of orange and red.

"This is beautiful, Seth." Felicity's eyes were wide with awe.

Seth was behind her, his arms holding her back against his chest. His chin rested on the top of her head. "It wouldn't be as perfect if you weren't here. I love you, Felicity Barrett."

"And I love you, Seth Tyler. I must be the luckiest woman alive." A sudden thought crossed her mind, and she smiled. Seth felt rather than saw the amusement.

"What is it, Felicity?" He lifted his head. "What are you thinking?"

Felicity's smile broadened. "I was just thinking of that old saying. You know, the one about finding love."

"Which saying?"

She leaned her head back contentedly. "Something like, love is found in the most unlikely places," she said. "I never thought it very wise until now."

Seth thought about that as the pine-scented evening breeze caressed their faces. Then his deep voice broke the stillness. "No, it's wrong. Love is found in the heart. That's the likeliest place of all."

Felicity nodded. She turned in his arms, her own heart filled with peace as he gathered her to him. She remained in his embrace until the sun disappeared, and the night air surrounded them.

"Come on, Felicity. Let's go in."

You'll flip . . . your pages won't!
Read paperbacks *hands-free* with

Book Mate · I

The perfect "mate" for all your romance paperbacks

Traveling • Vacationing • At Work • In Bed • Studying
• Cooking • Eating

Perfect size for all standard paperbacks, this wonderful invention makes reading a pure pleasure! Ingenious design holds paperback books OPEN and FLAT so even wind can't ruffle pages – leaves your hands free to do other things. Reinforced, wipe-clean vinyl-covered holder flexes to let you turn pages without undoing the strap . . . supports paperbacks so well, they have the strength of hardcovers!

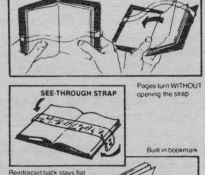

Pages turn WITHOUT opening the strap

SEE-THROUGH STRAP

Reinforced back stays flat

Built in bookmark

BOOK MARK

BACK COVER HOLDING STRIP

10 x 7¼ opened
Snaps closed for easy carrying, too

Available now. Send your name, address, and zip code, along with a check or money order for just $5.95 + 75¢ for delivery (for a total of $6.70) payable to Reader Service to:

Reader Service
Bookmate Offer
3010 Walden Avenue
P.O. Box 1396
Buffalo, N.Y. 14269-1396

Offer not available in Canada
*New York residents add appropriate sales tax.

BM-GR

PASSPORT TO ROMANCE VACATION SWEEPSTAKES

OFFICIAL RULES

SWEEPSTAKES RULES AND REGULATIONS. NO PURCHASE NECESSARY.
HOW TO ENTER:

1. To enter, complete this official entry form and return with your invoice in the envelope provided, or print your name, address, telephone number and age on a plain piece of paper and mail to: Passport to Romance, P.O. Box #1397, Buffalo, N.Y. 14269-1397. No mechanically reproduced entries accepted.

2. All entries must be received by the Contest Closing Date, midnight, December 31, 1990 to be eligible.

3. Prizes: There will be ten (10) Grand Prizes awarded, each consisting of a choice of a trip for two people to: i) London, England (approximate retail value $5,050 U.S.); ii) England, Wales and Scotland (approximate retail value $6,400 U.S.); iii) Caribbean Cruise (approximate retail value $7,300 U.S.); iv) Hawaii (approximate retail value $ 9,550 U.S.); v) Greek Island Cruise in the Mediterranean (approximate retail value $12,250 U.S.); vi) France (approximate retail value $7,300 U.S.).

4. Any winner may choose to receive any trip or a cash alternative prize of $5,000.00 U.S. in lieu of the trip.

5. Odds of winning depend on number of entries received.

6. A random draw will be made by Nielsen Promotion Services, an independent judging organization on January 29, 1991, in Buffalo, N.Y., at 11:30 a.m. from all eligible entries received on or before the Contest Closing Date. Any Canadian entrants who are selected must correctly answer a time-limited, mathematical skill-testing question in order to win. Quebec residents may submit any litigation respecting the conduct and awarding of a prize in this contest to the Régie des loteries et courses du Québec.

7. Full contest rules may be obtained by sending a stamped, self-addressed envelope to: "Passport to Romance Rules Request", P.O. Box 9998, Saint John, New Brunswick, E2L 4N4.

8. Payment of taxes other than air and hotel taxes is the sole responsibility of the winner.

9. Void where prohibited by law.

PASSPORT TO ROMANCE VACATION SWEEPSTAKES

OFFICIAL RULES

SWEEPSTAKES RULES AND REGULATIONS. NO PURCHASE NECESSARY.
HOW TO ENTER:

1. To enter, complete this official entry form and return with your invoice in the envelope provided, or print your name, address, telephone number and age on a plain piece of paper and mail to: Passport to Romance, P.O. Box #1397, Buffalo, N.Y. 14269-1397. No mechanically reproduced entries accepted.

2. All entries must be received by the Contest Closing Date, midnight, December 31, 1990 to be eligible.

3. Prizes: There will be ten (10) Grand Prizes awarded, each consisting of a choice of a trip for two people to: i) London, England (approximate retail value $5,050 U.S.); ii) England, Wales and Scotland (approximate retail value $6,400 U.S.); iii) Caribbean Cruise (approximate retail value $7,300 U.S.); iv) Hawaii (approximate retail value $ 9,550 U.S.); v) Greek Island Cruise in the Mediterranean (approximate retail value $12,250 U.S.); vi) France (approximate retail value $7,300 U.S.).

4. Any winner may choose to receive any trip or a cash alternative prize of $5,000.00 U.S. in lieu of the trip.

5. Odds of winning depend on number of entries received.

6. A random draw will be made by Nielsen Promotion Services, an independent judging organization on January 29, 1991, in Buffalo, N.Y., at 11:30 a.m. from all eligible entries received on or before the Contest Closing Date. Any Canadian entrants who are selected must correctly answer a time-limited, mathematical skill-testing question in order to win. Quebec residents may submit any litigation respecting the conduct and awarding of a prize in this contest to the Régie des loteries et courses du Québec.

7. Full contest rules may be obtained by sending a stamped, self-addressed envelope to: "Passport to Romance Rules Request", P.O. Box 9998, Saint John, New Brunswick, E2L 4N4.

8. Payment of taxes other than air and hotel taxes is the sole responsibility of the winner.

9. Void where prohibited by law.

RLS-DIR

PASSPORT TO ROMANCE
WIN 1 of 10 Vacations SEE INSIDE

VACATION SWEEPSTAKES

Official Entry Form

MONTH 2 ENTRY

Yes, enter me in the drawing for one of ten Vacations-for-Two! If I'm a winner, I'll get my choice of any of the six different destinations being offered — and I won't have to decide until after I'm notified!

Return entries with invoice in envelope provided along with Daily Travel Allowance Voucher. Each book in your shipment has two entry forms — and the more you enter, the better your chance of winning!

Name _____

Address _____ Apt. _____

City _____ State/Prov. _____ Zip/Postal Code _____

Daytime phone number _____
                            Area Code

☐ I am enclosing a Daily Travel Allowance Voucher in the amount of **$**_____ Write in amount revealed beneath scratch-off

© 1990 HARLEQUIN ENTERPRISES LTD

PASSPORT TO ROMANCE
WIN 1 of 10 Vacations SEE INSIDE

VACATION SWEEPSTAKES

Official Entry Form

MONTH 2 ENTRY

Yes, enter me in the drawing for one of ten Vacations-for-Two! If I'm a winner, I'll get my choice of any of the six different destinations being offered — and I won't have to decide until after I'm notified!

Return entries with invoice in envelope provided along with Daily Travel Allowance Voucher. Each book in your shipment has two entry forms — and the more you enter, the better your chance of winning!

Name _____

Address _____ Apt. _____

City _____ State/Prov. _____ Zip/Postal Code _____

Daytime phone number _____
                            Area Code

☐ I am enclosing a Daily Travel Allowance Voucher in the amount of **$**_____ Write in amount revealed beneath scratch-off

CPS-TWO